WHITECOTT MANOR

Emma Jane

Alistair Ellis is the proud gardener for beautiful fifteenth-century Whitecott Manor, in England's West Country. His life changes forever following a gas explosion at the manor, in which his boss—and love of his life—dies. However, his boss hasn't exactly gone for good and Alistair still finds himself involved in conversations with the deceased.

Circumstances improve when he meets Noah, the handsome dog groomer for the manor's new owners. Although there are some issues: Noah is already engaged and Alistair suffers from cynophobia—an acute fear of dogs!

Published by
NineStar Press
PO Box 91792
Albuquerque, New Mexico, 87199
www.ninestarpress.com

Print ISBN # 978-1-947139-84-8
Cover by Natasha Snow
Edited by Sam Lamb

*In memory of my grandfather, and best friend Emma, who both
passed away during the writing of this novel*

Chapter One

ONCE I WAS aware of the cuts, they stung like a bitch. I should've worn gloves, really, but it's so much easier not to. I was almost finished anyway, and the Harpers' rose borders were nearly ready. They'd look beautiful when they flowered in the summer—they always did. White and red rose blooms flanked the path to the tennis court. I just had one last bush to prune and then I could stop for a cuppa. The cuts were itching now too, right where the thorns had snagged and ripped my skin. I sucked the flesh between my thumb and index finger, tasting blood and mud, and stood there, secateurs in hand, watching the house.

It was a fifteenth-century manor—a beautiful listed building made from warm-yellow stone. It'd been revamped inside, a strange mixture of modern and ancient, and was currently—unfortunately, in my opinion—on the market. I didn't want it to sell; I didn't want to lose my job. The Harpers assured me that whoever bought the place would keep me on but, well, it wasn't down to them.

I took my hand from my mouth and watched as the estate agent led a middle-aged couple from their car—some sort of old classic; light blue with a soft-top—to the front of the manor. Even at this distance, I could see the look on their faces as they gazed up at the building before entering. They loved it already. Everybody did; it was such an impressive place. Bloody hell, I'd buy it if I had a spare eight million lying around.

I glowered to myself and turned back to the last bush, reaching into the branches to snip it into some sort of order. I cut myself on another thorn and swore impatiently.

"Language."

I turned to see Mr Harper—Emmett—watching me. He stood there, smiling, his hands tucked in the pockets of his ridiculous purple corduroys. He always reminded me of Colin Firth, though he didn't look particularly like him. He was a similar age, I suppose, and had that same clipped accent and no-nonsense manner.

I tossed rose clippings into my wheelbarrow. "Sorry. It's these roses. They're full of thorns."

"Ah, the roses. Yes. I thought perhaps you'd spotted Mr Daniels showing the Scrantons around."

"Scrantons?"

"Mr and Mrs Scranton. I don't know their first names, and I don't care. Lottery winners, apparently."

I scratched at my cheek with the edge of my thumbnail and then wiped the back of my hand across my brow. "You really want Whitecott Manor bought by lottery winners?" I asked. It wasn't really any of my business, but I didn't want to see the place sold on yet again because the Scrantons squandered all their money and ended up bankrupt within a year.

Emmett shrugged. "My dear, I don't care who buys it as long as they cough up the money. You know I can't afford to keep the place."

I knew. Emmett was swimming in debt. His daughters—all five of them—had now moved out and he had to pay for everything on his own since his wife had left. Old Mrs Harper, Emmett's mother, lived in the house with him, but she was in her eighties and, I think, had about as much money as he did. They wanted to move to a little cottage somewhere, with a nice granny annex and a garden that didn't require much attention. Certainly not enough attention to take me with them.

I hadn't said anything. Emmett came and put his hand to the small of my back. "Whoever ends up here would be mad to let you go. They can see how beautiful the gardens are."

I nodded and stared into the rose bush.

"And you're beautiful," he added. "Who would not want you around?"

"You don't need to flatter me." I snipped at the bush and tossed branches into my wheelbarrow.

Emmett chuckled and moved away. "Cheer up, Alistair! You've got your whole life ahead of you. I'm off to take Mother her tea."

I watched him stroll back to the house as if he didn't have a care in the world. I'd miss him most of all. Well, maybe he wouldn't move far. I'd probably still see him around—at the local fair or plant show perhaps. Besides, house sales took ages; I knew that from experience. If the Scrantons bought the place, it'd be a while yet before they moved in. And if they decided they didn't want a gardener—*if*—then I had plenty of time to look for a new job. I could always audition for the X Factor and see where that got me—Emmett said I had a great singing voice, and I'd often dreamed of performing on stage.

I picked up the wheelbarrow and went to empty the clippings on the compost heap. I was just trundling back to the roses when I spotted the estate agent leading the Scrantons out into the gardens. I'd make myself scarce; I didn't want to have to smile politely while they stood and gawked, so I downed tools and headed to the potting shed.

The cabbage seedlings were coming on nicely, I noticed, but my beetroots were depressingly small. I'd never had much luck with beetroot. They never grew much larger than rat testicles. I shrugged out of my overalls and tied the arms around my waist, singing an Elvis track softly beneath my breath.

I'd just reached for a watering can when an almighty bang made me jump out of my skin. The windows blew out the front of the manor, followed by tongues of fire licking the frames. I stared, heart frozen and mouth open. Then my heart started again, blood thumping in my ears. I threw open the shed door and ran.

"Emmett!"

I dashed towards the building, pulled open the door, and hurried down the hall to where the explosion had come from—the kitchen. Flames crackled in the room, red and angry and louder than I would've expected. Smoke and heat billowed outwards, and I coughed and covered my nose. My eyes watered.

"Emmett!" I yelled again.

Something crashed—maybe part of the ceiling falling—and I took a step to go after Emmett when somebody grabbed my arm and hauled me back.

"Mr Harper's in there," I shouted at the estate agent, fighting the man's vice-like grip. "Emmett! *Emmett!*"

The estate agent pulled me away, forcing me bodily back down the hall and outside. He was speaking—shouting, I think—but I yelled too, my voice hoarse, and I couldn't hear him, couldn't see, couldn't... *Emmett.*

Sirens screamed in the distance, and then I saw the lights flashing through the trees that flanked the lane beside the manor. Fire engines arrived in a cacophony of noise and colour. The estate agent held me in a bear hug, and all I could do as firefighters jumped from their vehicles was stare at the flames roaring from the broken windows.

THE FUNERAL TOOK place a week later. It was hot—too hot for spring—and I was sweaty and uncomfortable in my black suit. A tree thick with pink blossoms hung over the grave, but Old Mrs Harper and her granddaughters occupied all the shade. I rolled my shoulders in an attempt to get the shirt material unstuck from my back and eyed the little black fan that Persephone Harper batted prettily around her face.

"It wouldn't suit you," Emmett said, rocking back on his heels as he stood by my side. "It'd make you look positively camp."

I hid my smile by bowing my head and staring at the patch of grass beneath my feet. Mr Harper's apparition first appeared to me a day after the fire—I suppose it was a weird sort of coping mechanism. The real Emmett Harper was currently being lowered into the ground, snug and lifeless in his mahogany coffin. I might've been going insane, but I *liked* having him with me. When I was a boy, I don't know, nine or ten years old, I had an imaginary friend called Peter. I remember I always had trouble picturing Peter's face, but with Emmett I could see him clearly. It could only be because I knew him—had known him—so well.

The vicar spoke, the daughters came forward with handfuls of dirt, and I stood there and smiled to myself as I remembered him. A blackbird twittered in the tree, its song far too cheerful for such a sombre occasion, and as I lifted my gaze, Emmett raised a shotgun and aimed it into the branches.

I bit back a laugh and managed to turn it into a half-cough, half-sneeze. Nobody noticed. Mourners moved away, and the Harpers spoke softly to the vicar. I followed the procession from the graveyard and around to the front of the church where people lingered to talk to one another.

"You horrible boy," Emmett said, leaning close to my ear. "Laughing at my funeral."

"I didn't laugh," I said.

The man standing in front of me turned, smiled, and said, "No, nor me. Well done us, eh? I always feel like laughing in these sorts of situations."

I wondered how many funerals he'd been to. He was around my age, I suppose. Late twenties. Nice-looking, if a little plain. Well spoken. He held out his hand, and I took it—his grip warm and firm.

"Martin Spencer," he said. "Mr Harper's solicitor."

"Alistair Ellis. Mr Harper's gardener."

"And lover," Emmett added. "Don't forget that."

Well, yes. Of course I wouldn't forget *that*, but I didn't think it appropriate to bring up in polite conversation. I scratched the back of my hand.

"Oh. Will you be looking for a new job?"

"Will I...?"

"I'm sure old Mrs Harper's told you about the sale. Should be nice and easy. The Scrantons keeping you on, are they?"

"I've not spoken to them," I said, frowning.

"Oh." Martin pretended somebody had called him and turned away with his hand raised. I glowered to myself. So Whitecott Manor was going to end up in the hands of the lottery winners. I hoped they were going to treat the place with the respect it deserved, and I especially hoped they *were* going to let me keep my job.

As I turned back to the graveyard, I spotted old Mrs Harper and her granddaughters making their way to the car park. Everybody would head to the village hall where the wake was to be held and fill themselves up on sausage rolls and finger sandwiches.

I couldn't face it. Not now. I slipped away without anybody noticing and headed to my car.

Chapter Two

I CARRIED ON working while builders carried out repairs on the manor house. First my wages came from old Mrs Harper, and then, once the sale had gone through, the Scrantons paid me, though I'd still not spoken to them. They had more important things to worry about, and I guess it was just convenient to keep the existing gardener. I'd seen Mr Scranton—David—a few times, keeping an eye on the repair work and making sure the builders weren't slacking off. Once he'd glanced in my direction, but I kept my head down and wheeled my trimmings off to the compost heap.

I knew I should've introduced myself, but he was just as capable at coming over to me. Besides, part of me was still indignant that these people were *lottery winners* and really didn't suit the place at all. Not like Emmett had.

I remembered when I'd first started working there. Emmett's wife had just left him for the previous gardener—who'd been fired a month earlier—and old Mrs Harper had hired me because she knew my father and, I was certain, knew I was gay and unlikely to show any interest in her daughter-in-law. By the time I started, young Mrs Harper had left anyway, leaving Emmett to brood alone in the garden. And watch me.

He'd sit on the white bench under the apple tree and read his newspaper. Every time I'd straighten up to rub my back—I was sowing carrot seeds at the time—I noticed he'd clear his throat and turn his attention back to the paper. It used to make me smile.

Then he would join me and ask questions about my work and ask after my father. It developed into little compliments—about the garden at first, I shaped the box hedges far nicer than the previous gardener— and then about me. I was a handsome young man and the like. He'd touch the small of my back, just lightly, and I really wanted him to take it further.

I didn't make the first move. I wasn't sure enough of his intentions and I didn't want to lose my job. But one day, he came to me in the potting shed. I remember turning as he opened the door and wondering what was going on as he wore an unusually serious expression. His breath smelled of alcohol as he said, "That's it. I've had quite enough of this."

He strode up to me and kissed me, and I probably should have asked if he was sure, because he was almost definitely drunk, but instead I ended up giving him a blow job.

I remember looking up at his face.

"You're getting awfully maudlin. And will you watch what you're doing? You're drowning those begonias."

I cursed and turned the hose off, stepping back out of the soggy patch I'd created in the border. Emmett laughed.

"Sorry," I mumbled. I shook water from my hands and reeled the hose in.

"You need some time off. Go and find yourself a holiday romance."

"*You* are dead," I said. "You don't get to give me time off any more."

"Then go and see a doctor because talking to yourself is clearly a sign of madness."

I sighed and rubbed my face. Bloody mental lunatic... A metallic clank coming from the direction of the house made me look up. The builders were removing the scaffolding and loading it back onto the lorry. Mr and Mrs Scranton would be resident any day now, and I would just have to deal with it.

ZARA—MRS SCRANTON, that is—was actually quite a nice lady. She'd bring me a tray of tea and biscuits while I worked and we'd stop and chat about what she wanted to do with the garden. Her two little Bichon Frise dogs, Candy and Coco, were a pain in the arse and would dig up and eat my bulbs before I could stop them.

David Scranton mostly glared at me as he stood outside and smoked his cigarettes. He barely spoke to me, unless it was to tell me about something he didn't like or wanted to change. I'd defer to Zara, and more often than not, she'd tell me to ignore him.

All in all, working for the Scrantons was all right. I missed Emmett, though his apparition stayed with me, and I visited old Mrs Harper fortnightly as she'd moved to a cottage in the village and I'd sneak her fruit from Whitecott Manor's orchard.

For weeks I did nothing but work. Then, one evening out of the blue, an old mate of mine—Freddie Carter who'd moved to London for some posh office job—appeared on my doorstep and told me we needed to catch up. We just went to the local pub for a bit of karaoke, but Freddie managed to hook up with a pretty blonde girl and I was left sitting at the table on my own, drinking my pint of Thatcher's cider.

Emmett dropped into the seat opposite me. "You, my boy, are wasting away. You've not been with anybody since me. I'm quite sure your testicles will shrivel up like prunes."

I slurped my drink and eyed Freddie with the woman. I didn't know for certain, but I was pretty sure I was the only gay man in the village. If I wanted to get laid, I'd have to head to a gay bar in one of the towns nearby.

"Or," Emmett said, "you could try Internet dating. I hear that's all the rage nowadays."

"I don't want a relationship," I said.

"Talking to yourself, Al?"

Freddie loomed over me, grinning inanely, one arm wrapped around the woman's waist. She giggled, leaned in to Freddie, and whispered something in his ear, to which he replied, loudly, "Nah, love. He's gay, this one. You tell your mate she can join us though, eh? If you fancy it."

"Fred," I muttered. I didn't want to hear about his sex life and I was sure the rest of the pub wouldn't, either. He gave my arm a playful jab and headed back to the bar with the woman. I downed the rest of my pint and sat there, feeling lonely and sorry for myself.

Internet dating. God help me.

BLOODY FREDDIE. I'D not really felt it until he'd dragged me out and now I couldn't stop thinking about it. It being—what else?—sex. Sex and the fact I was all alone in my little house in rural Somerset. My dad visited me, of course, and I'd still go to his for our traditional Sunday lunch. Then there were my trips to see old Mrs Harper and my garden chats with Zara, but I was lacking in male company. The imaginary ghost of my dead boss didn't quite count—nor did the passing grunt of communication from David.

I was busy treating the wood of the summer house, humming a song I couldn't remember the name of, when a white van pulled up in the driveway, tyres crunching the gravel. The cursive lettering on the side of the van read: Mucky Mutts. My heart thumped. Mutts meant dogs. If there were giant, drooling, snarling beasts in that van, I needed to get out of the way, quick. Coco and Candy I could just about cope with, but anything else... I almost turned to go, but as the driver got out I couldn't help but watch him.

Dark hair, dark eyes, and dark skin. He was slender and lovely and, quite obviously, gay.

Chapter Three

I WATCHED WITH the paintbrush paused in my hand halfway to the wall of the summerhouse as the man closed the van door and walked towards the house. He wore dark trousers and a plain blue T-shirt that had some sort of small logo on it that I couldn't read from where I stood. I don't think he noticed me at all, and he carried on up to the doorstep, a cute little swagger in his walk. The dogs barked inside the manor when he rang the doorbell, and a moment later, Zara opened the door.

"Close your mouth," Emmett said, appearing by my side. "You're practically drooling."

The man disappeared inside, so I turned back to the summerhouse and bent to dip my brush in the little pot of varnish. "Jealous?" I asked.

"Of a dog groomer? Hardly. Besides, he's just a boy. And far too pretty for you."

I brushed aside a spider crawling across the wood and slapped on the varnish. "You always told me I was beautiful."

"My dear, you were always the most beautiful flower in my garden."

I painted quietly for a while and Emmett wandered off. I wasn't disrespecting his memory by looking at another man. And it wouldn't hurt if I just spoke to him. Just to say hello. The varnish ended up a little slapdash as I hurried to finish. Once I'd put the pot away and left the brush to soak in some turps, I snatched up my hoe and headed to the driveway to do a bit of weeding around the borders.

The sun shone, although it wasn't overly warm, and I used it as an excuse to shrug out of the top half of my overalls and tie the arms around my waist, leaving my white vest top exposed. Emmett had always told me I had lovely arms—I knew they were my best feature. It came from all the manual labour. Hopefully, they would attract the attentions of the dog groomer.

I was just skimming weeds when the front door opened and the man exited the manor. Zara stood in the doorway with one of the dogs in her arms, and she caught my eye and flashed me a smile before heading back inside.

I pretended to be more interested in my work, though I was very close to his van. I nodded as he approached and said, "Afternoon."

He smiled, and I noticed his gaze travel over my body as he replied, "Hiya." He dropped his aitch.

I cleared my throat. "You're something to do with the dogs, are you?" It was a stupid question, but it was all I could think of.

"I will be. Mrs Scranton wanted to check me out and see how I got on with the pooches before she'll let me clip them. I passed, so I'll be back next week for our first appointment." He smiled again. His bone structure was amazing. He honestly looked like one of those male models or a footballer or something. I couldn't place his accent—he wasn't local—he sounded Northern, maybe.

"Oh right," I said. "Well, I'll probably be around."

He laughed at that and opened the van door. "Good to know!" Then he smiled at me again and got into the driver's seat. I was still staring after him as he drove away.

I DIDN'T EVEN know his name. What a bloody idiot! I had to wait a week for him to be back—provided he came back when I was working—and then what? I'd make a prat out of myself again. How often did bichons need grooming? How many chances would I get to speak with him?

Of course, the first thing I did when I returned home was google dog grooming. Bichons needed clipping every four to eight weeks. I thought about Coco and Candy. They were pretty hairy; it'd probably be every four weeks for them. Maybe two weeks.

I typed Mucky Mutts into the search engine and scrolled through the various dog groomers until I found him. Mucky Mutts of Yeovil, Somerset. That had to be him, and yep, when I clicked into the site, the first thing I saw was a photo of him standing behind a dog grooming... table...thing, with a pair of scissors in hand as he concentrated on the...some sort of spaniel.

I scratched my face. I wasn't very good at dog breeds. In fact, I tended to avoid dogs as much as was possible. He was clearly a dog lover, though, and I wondered if I should learn some of the names.

"Labrador," Emmett offered. "Good dogs."

"I know what a Labrador is," I said, squinting at the pictures. "But look at this hairy thing here, it looks like a mop. I don't want him thinking I'm thick."

"And do you think he knows the names of the plants?"

That was a very good point, and besides, I was getting carried away with myself. I clicked on his About Me page and found his name. Noah. He'd not put his surname, but that didn't matter. It wasn't like I was going to marry the guy.

"Just a quick fuck in the potting shed," Emmett said.

I smirked. I'd always loved it when he swore—his accent made it sound so much dirtier.

"Look at him," I said, gazing at the photo. "Why is someone that good-looking not on the TV? He could be... I don't know. A celebrity dog groomer. Then he'd be in all the magazines and he'd end up shirtless in the Gay Times."

"My dear, you're drooling again," Emmett said.

"Oh, come on," I said, waving a hand at the photo. "Don't say you wouldn't!"

"I only ever had eyes for you."

Emmett moved away from the computer and sat on my sofa. A pang of guilt touched my guts and then turned into loss before it passed. Truth was, I didn't know if Emmett had ever looked at another man, before me or during our time together. We hadn't socialised—it wasn't as if Emmett was out of the closet. Come to think of it, I wasn't sure he was even gay. I mean, yes, we slept together, so clearly he liked men, but I knew he'd loved his wife.

"Can't a man have both?" Emmett asked.

"Of course." I switched the computer off, deciding I'd have a cup of tea before heading over to see Emmett's mother. I wanted to ask after Persephone—the last time I'd visited, she'd been there and had been telling anybody who'd listen—mostly me, as I suspect old Mrs Harper had selective hearing—about her new man. A man named Joe Scranton.

"And why does that matter?" Emmett asked.

"He's twice her age."

Emmett raised his eyebrows. I was being hypocritical, I know. Mr Harper was—had been—much older than myself. I didn't know why it bothered me, Persephone's love life was nothing to do with me, and God knows I had no interest in it, but...there was something I didn't like.

I WALKED THROUGH the village to old Mrs Harper's cottage, passing my father's work van on the way. He'd parked outside the pub, and I had no idea whether he was working in there or having a crafty pint. A quick look at my watch told me it was five p.m., so there was a good chance he'd gone in there for something to eat. Dad didn't cook much since Mum died, other than the traditional roast, and without the pub, he probably would've existed solely on microwave meals.

"Maybe you should be seeing to your father rather than my mother," Emmett said. He strolled beside me, ridiculous and handsome in a green tweed suit.

"Maybe," I muttered. My dad didn't like a fuss, didn't like me worrying. We cared about each other, loved each other, but expressing emotions? That was something Mum had done. She'd fussed over the pair of us. Without her, we didn't really know how to behave around each other.

I scratched the side of my nose, glanced down the road to check nothing was coming, and crossed over to the green. The oak tree, big and beautiful in the middle of the lawn, had a scattering of black and twisted leaves surrounding it. I squinted up into the branches and noticed a white powder coating some of the leaves—oak mildew. A good spray with a fungicide would fix that, and I pondered contacting the council to get them onto it as I neared the little row of cottages on the far side of the green.

The light shone through the window of old Mrs Harper's cottage though it wasn't dark out, and I could see her moving about behind the net curtain. I made my way down the path and knocked on the door, waiting for longer than usual for her to answer. When she did, she soon ushered me inside.

"Alistair. Good. I need someone to look at this blasted television."

She turned inside, leaving me on the doorstep to follow. I closed the door behind me and headed into the living room. The television screen showed nothing but static.

"Harriet," old Mrs Harper said, waving a hand. "She fiddled with it earlier, and now the damned thing won't work."

"Harriet was here?" I tried not to sound surprised and failed. Harriet, Emmett's oldest daughter, lived in London and only came to this neck of the woods when she had to.

"Yes, yes. Fix that, will you?" Old Mrs Harper wandered out of the room, and I heard her bustling about in the kitchen.

I picked up the remote control and pressed buttons until the TV came back on to the right setting. I wanted to ask what Harriet wanted, but it wasn't my place.

"What does Harriet ever want?" Emmett asked, appearing on the sofa. "Money. She married that awful banker for his money."

Old Mrs Harper came into the room carrying a tea tray, and I hurried to take it from her. "Was Harriet okay?" I asked as she lowered herself onto the sofa next to Emmett. I put the tray on the coffee table and poured tea for the both of us.

"Hm? Oh, yes, I suppose so. She's still not happy the manor sold for so little, but there's not a lot we can do about that."

I sat in the armchair and sipped my tea. Old Mrs Harper noticed the TV worked again, and she jabbed at the remote control to turn it off. "Thank you, Alistair. Oh, Alistair? You're not still gay, are you?"

"'Fraid so," I said.

The old lady sagged in her chair, hugging her teacup between her hands. "Pity," she said. "You'd be a much better match for Persephone than that Scranton fellow."

I very nearly spat out my tea but managed to almost choke myself on it instead. Once I'd finished coughing, I said, "You're not a fan of Joe Scranton, then?"

"Is anyone? He's one of those...what do you young people call them? Chaps."

I frowned. "What chaps?"

"Chaps," she repeated, as if that made her any clearer. "You know. One of the *lower classes*."

"Oh! Chavs." I smirked to myself as I pictured Joe Scranton. Aesthetically, I could see the appeal. A square jaw covered in designer stubble and a body that could melt ice. Personality wise, well, I got the impression he was a bit of a lad. "He's just a bit rough around the edges."

I said it to convince myself as much as old Mrs Harper. She snorted over her teacup, and as our gazes met, I knew neither of us believed it.

Chapter Four

MY DAD LIVED in a little two-up two-down on a cul-de-sac full of houses that all looked the same. One of the neighbours had a birthday party that weekend, and the road was full of cars and the street busy with children kicking a football. I squeezed onto the driveway behind my dad's van and, after switching off the engine, sat in my car for a while staring into space.

Topics floated through my mind and vanished before I could turn them into something interesting. What would we talk about this time? God, I hated small talk.

I left my car, glanced across the road as a cheer rang out from the house with the *Happy Tenth Birthday!* banner across the door, and made my way up the garden path. I knocked and entered without waiting for a reply—my dad knew I was coming, so the door was unlocked.

The smell of roast chicken wafted down the hall, and my stomach rumbled. "Dad?" I called.

He was in the kitchen, his back to the door as he cut up a turnip and tossed the pieces into a saucepan. He half turned to me. "All right, son?"

I nodded. "You?"

"Ah." My father had a strong West Country accent, like a few of the older residents still had around the village, and although his response might've baffled anybody else, I grew up knowing 'ah' meant 'yes.' I nodded again and stood in the doorway with my hands in my pockets.

"Smells good," I said.

"Ready in about half an hour," he replied. "Sit down, will 'ee? Standing in the doorway like that, you make the place look proper untidy."

I pulled out a chair, wincing at the creak as it slid over the linoleum, and sat at the table. Dad continued chopping up turnip until it had all disappeared into the pan, and then he wiped his hands on a tea towel. I wished Emmett were with me, but he'd abandoned me—or, I was unable to imagine him—and I was stuck there all alone with nothing to say.

I cleared my throat. "Old Mrs Harper was asking after you," I said.

"Oh ah?"

"Yeah."

"All right, is she?"

"Yeah."

More awkward silence. Dad opened the oven and a waft of heat and roast chicken hit me in the face. I almost said 'smells good' again until I remembered I'd already used that one. I excused myself from the table to use the bathroom, even though I didn't need to go, and managed to pass five minutes attempting to remove the dirt from beneath my nails. When I returned to the kitchen, Dad had made us both a cup of tea, and mine sat steaming in my place.

"What's it like working for they new owners up at the manor then? That Mr Scranton still a miserable sod?"

I smiled. Whitecott Manor was our main topic of conversation, and every weekend since the Scrantons had moved in, my dad had asked what it was like to work for them. "Still doesn't talk to me much," I said. "But I don't mind. Zara's nice."

"That his missus?"

"Yeah."

"They still got all that wood panelling in the reception room?"

"I think so," I said.

"I helped restore that back when I did odd jobs for old Mrs Harper."

I already knew that, of course, and I suspected my dad knew I knew that, but I appreciated the attempt at conversation, and so I said, "I can ask Zara if you can come and have a look around, if you like?"

"Nah."

I drummed my fingers on the table and was pleased when Dad dished up the dinner and placed it in front of me. We sat at opposite ends of the table and ate in silence except for one "These roast potatoes are lovely" from me, and a "Pass the salt, Al?" from him. When we both finished, we sat for a while, letting the food go down, until we stood to wash the dishes and clear up. I imagined Mum looking down on us, wanting to bang our heads together.

I don't know why conversation had gotten so awkward between us. We were just stuck.

I STOOD IN the greenhouse, eating my cheese and pickle sandwich as rain splashed into the pond. An attractive pair of waders covered the lower half of my body, and I was hot and sticky despite the weather. As soon as I finished my lunch, and hopefully the rain would've stopped by then, I'd be back out there, wading into the pond to finish skimming the weed. The pond was large and full of ornamental koi and water lilies. Mrs Scranton had a gaudy statue of a naked woman, gold-coloured, installed at the centre. It dribbled water into the pond from a vase the woman carried.

Emmett appeared outside the greenhouse, blocking my view. He held a black umbrella above his head, and water dripped down around him from the material. I smiled at my impressive imagination—the details were always spot on—and raised a hand in greeting.

"Can't you do something about that statue?" he asked, his voice raised to reach me through the rain and glass. "Bloody awful thing. I'm sure it can meet with some sort of accident if you try hard enough."

"Zara likes it," I said. "You have to let it go."

Emmett's brow creased into a frown, and then we both turned towards the manor at the sound of tyres munching up the gravel driveway. I spotted the white van, mud splashed up the side, and dropped my sandwich to grab my umbrella from where it leaned against the door.

"Don't make a fool of yourself," Emmett called after me as I jogged across the lawn to the van.

I reached it just as the driver door opened, and I stood there, umbrella at the ready, as Noah looked up at me.

"Hiya," he said, smiling. "You waiting for me or something?"

"No!" I waved a hand at my waders. "I was working. Saw you coming and had an umbrella to hand so...um..."

Noah got out of the van and shimmied into the space in front of me so he could benefit from the umbrella. He had beautiful dark eyes. "I'm Noah," he said.

"Alistair," I replied, pleased I hadn't replied with 'I know.'

"Giz a hand, will you?"

He hurried to the back of the van, and I followed him, keeping the brolly over his head as if I was the footman.

"There's no dogs in there, is there?" I asked. "I mean...they're not going to jump out when you open the door?"

"Don't be daft." He pulled the doors open and dragged out a folded-up table, a metal pole contraption that looked dangerous, and a couple of dog leads.

"Grab my bag?" he asked, and I did before rushing after him towards the manor.

We stood under the portico, and I ditched the umbrella as Noah rang the bell. "I should get back to work," I said.

"You can't help me carry it all in, can you?"

The door opened, and Zara stood before us, one of the little white dogs in her arms. The other stood behind her, looking wary, one paw held up. It gruffed and then scurried away.

"Hiya," Noah said. "Where do you want me?"

Zara waved him inside and gave him instructions to one of the rooms down the hall. She turned back to me and jabbed a finger at my waders. "Take those off before you come in here!"

"I wasn't... I was going to..."

Zara tutted and sauntered after Noah, leaving me standing. I shrugged out of the waders and boots and left it all in the portico. My left sock had a hole in, I noticed, and my big toe stuck out. Groaning, I picked up Noah's bag and headed down the hallway to find him. He'd already set up the table, and Zara was securing her dog to the pole when I entered the room.

"I'll bring in Coco once you're done with this little one," Zara said. She kissed the dog's head, made baby talk, and then flashed me a wink and left me alone with Noah.

Noah took the bag out of my hand and jerked his head at the room. "Nice this, innit? Dead posh."

We were in what had been Emmett's study, only his old mahogany desk had been replaced with cardboard boxes the Scranton's hadn't yet unpacked. The large window with its sand-coloured stone frame looked out over the formal gardens. Box hedging marked triangular bedding areas of soft, herbaceous planting, interspaced with pathways leading to the centre of the design and a seating area. I spied one of the topiary cones looking a little wonky from this angle and made a mental note to get the shears on it.

Noah was fussing the dog. The metal pole fit to the table, a lead dangled from it and around the dog's neck, reminding me of a hangman's noose. Emmett appeared on the window seat and made a daft choking action which made me chuckle.

"What?" Noah asked.

"Hm? Oh...thinking of something that happened earlier. So, I guess I should leave you to it." I'd frozen to the spot, though, not wanting to leave and yet not wanting to get any closer to the dog.

"You can't giz a hand, could you?"

That made my heart pound again. I didn't want to touch the dog. I couldn't touch the dog. What if it sensed my fear and attacked me? The two little dogs always gruffed at me whenever they were in the garden—I think they knew I didn't like them.

"Just come here and hold her head." Noah bent to take a pair of clippers and a comb from his bag and then raised his eyebrows at me once he straightened up and saw I hadn't moved.

My gaze flicked to Emmett and back again. "I'm allergic," I said. God, that was a good excuse. I smiled.

"Oh." Noah shrugged, turned on the clippers and, holding the dog with one hand, got to work.

I stood there, stupefied, as he ran the clippers expertly over the dog's body, lifting its legs and moving its head as he worked. White fur fell away in neat tufts. His movements mesmerised me—*he* mesmerised me, and I felt strangely calm until I noticed the ring on his finger.

"You're married?" I asked.

I think I sounded confused because he grinned at me. "Engaged. Tony. Six months now."

I could only nod. After a moment, I turned to leave, but Noah spoke again. "How about you? Anyone special in your life? Girlfriend?" He flashed me another smile as he added, "Boyfriend?"

"No. No boyfriend. Or girlfriend. No...uh. I'm single. Nobody really special. I mean, there was, but..." I glanced towards Emmett.

"Like that, is it? Tough luck." Noah snipped around the dog's muzzle with a pair of scissors and then threw me a look. "Thought you'd be sneezing. What with your allergies."

"It's more of a rash...situation," I said. "You know. If I touch them." I cleared my throat and moved towards the door, realising I had to get back to work, and I wasn't doing myself any favours by standing there, staring at somebody else's man.

"Alistair," Noah said as my hand touched the door handle. "What time do you get off? Could go for a drink later, if you fancy it."

"Yeah?" I smiled. "With you and Tony?"

Noah laughed. "Just me. I thought we could get to know each other as we're kinda working together now. Tony'll be working late anyway."

I loved the way he pronounced 'thought.' Faught. I wanted to tease him about it. Instead I said, "Okay. I finish about six, but I can meet you in the King's Arms at eight? That's the pub in the middle of the village."

"All right. Catch you later then."

I stepped out into the hallway, glanced about for the other dog, and then headed for the door with a stupid grin on my face. I stopped in my tracks when the big door opened and David entered, sopping wet and already peeling off his coat. He paused when he saw me.

"What are you doing in here?" he asked, turning briefly to hang his coat on the stand.

"Mr Scranton. I was just helping the dog guy with his table and—"

"You shouldn't be in here. Nothing to do with you in here. Get out."

I raised my eyebrows at his rudeness but shrugged it off and made for the door. David grabbed my arm as I passed and held it tight. He moved his face, red with water dripping from the tip of his nose, close to mine. "I don't want to see you in here again."

"Zara didn't mind."

He opened his mouth as if to reply. Instead he let me go and grunted a response. Frowning, I headed outside.

"Awful man," Emmett said, appearing by my side under the portico as the door closed behind me. "I wonder what he wanted to say?"

"I don't know," I said, grabbing my waders. "And I don't care."

Chapter Five

AFTER WORK, I returned home to shower and shave and put on my best clothes while reminding myself I wasn't going on a date. I sang Karma Chameleon loudly, which was unusually camp and upbeat for me. Emmett watched me as I threw various shirts onto my bed, and when I turned to grin at him, he folded his arms and glowered.

"You'll make a fool of yourself," he said.

"Look, I'm just going for a good time. I've been miserable since you died, and bored, and I need a night out. I *know* Noah's unattainable, okay? Not even a quick shag. Besides, even if he wasn't engaged, it wouldn't work between us. He likes dogs! And I'm...allergic."

I picked up a salmon-coloured shirt and held it up for Emmett's inspection. He shook his head and waved a hand at my white one with the blue flowers. My mother had bought me that shirt just before she'd died.

Melancholy bubbled up inside me, numbing everything and making Emmett disappear until I picked up the shirt and put it on. I buttoned it in front of the mirror and smiled when Emmett stood behind me.

"It brings out your eyes," he said.

"Mum always knew what suited me."

"You'll make that boy realise he's getting married far too young," Emmett said. He laughed. "Is that your plan? You'll go and show him what he's missing out on."

"I don't have a *plan*. I told you. I'm going for a good time."

"Of course you are, my dear boy," Emmett said, and I smiled.

EVERY ONCE IN a while the King's Arms held a live music night. As I strolled down the road towards the pub, I spotted the blackboard outside the door advertising the band playing. A band called The Honey Badgers. I couldn't decide whether that was a good thing or a bad thing.

Not the band's name, although that struck me as daft, but the fact a band was playing at all. Would Noah and I be able to hear one another? Did that matter? It would be an opportunity to get close to him if anything, to lean close to him so he could hear me, to laugh, to touch…

I shook my head at myself and went inside. The usual people propped up the bar, and I gave a polite nod to a couple of my dad's old mates before leaning against the bar to order a drink. Noah hadn't arrived, so I stayed where I was in full sight of the door.

The pub had music playing, some sort of generic pop CD, but I could see the band setting up for their performance at the back of the room, fiddling with lighting and amps and microphones. God, I'd loved to have joined them and belted out a couple of tunes.

I slurped my cider, wiped moisture from my lips, and glanced towards the door again. I imagined Noah would be the only nonwhite person there tonight—Mr Chan from the local Chinese takeaway didn't strike me as the sort of person who'd like live music—and I worried suddenly that he'd feel awkward. Then I worried that that thought somehow made me racist.

"You're not a racist," Emmett said, perching on a bar stool. I noticed he'd dressed up for the occasion too, though he looked like someone out of Downton Abbey.

"You can't be here," I told him. "You'll put me off! I can't be talking to you like some sort of nutcase."

"I'm here for support until your date arrives." He turned from me to wave to the barman, who, of course, ignored him.

"It's not a date."

"Of course not." Emmett attempted to flag down the barman and failed once again. He sighed. "What does one have to do to get some service around here?"

I frowned. "I don't know. Breathe? Have a heartbeat? Actually exist, maybe?"

"You're being flippant, Alistair, and it doesn't suit you."

With a resigned sigh, I raised my glass to my lips. I had to ignore Emmett if I didn't want Noah to think I was completely insane. Maybe alcohol would help.

The door opened and a young couple entered. My shoulders sagged in disappointment until somebody else followed them in.

Noah wore black jeans and a striped V-neck top that served to make his chest look broader than it probably was. He looked around until he spotted me, and when he did, his face broke into a smile. I raised my hand in greeting and he headed over.

"Hiya," he said. "Hope I'm not late."

"I'm probably early," I replied. "Didn't have so far to come as you." I pulled my gaze away from him and beckoned the barman over. "Can I get you a drink?"

"Just a lemonade for me, ta," Noah said. "Driving."

We stood in a semi awkward silence while the barman served the drink. I paid and then waved a hand towards the tables. "Shall we sit? There's a band playing tonight. Do you like music?"

Noah laughed and followed me over to the table. "Oh yeah, love music, me. Are there people who don't like music?"

"I meant live music." I hadn't meant to sound like an idiot. I cleared my throat and glanced towards the bar, where Emmett was still trying to be served.

"S'all right, I s'pose," Noah said. I noticed how he briefly watched the band with only a vague expression of interest on his face. When his gaze met mine again, he smiled. "My little sister's a performer."

"Oh yeah?"

He nodded. "She did this drag king act up in Manchester. Trying to get some interest going somewhere 'round here. Bristol maybe. She's dead good."

I paused with my cider halfway to my lips. "Drag... what?"

"King," Noah said. "You know. Like a drag queen, except she's a woman who dresses up like a man."

"Oh."

"He's called Johnny Hammers."

"Who is?"

"My little sister!"

I almost said 'oh' again. My lips formed the shape, but I made myself take a drink instead so I didn't look like an idiot. Noah laughed.

"You're funny, you are," he said.

I smiled. "Am I?"

Noah nodded. He seemed about to say more, but the lead singer of the band tapped the microphone and introduced himself and his mates to the room. I clapped, and Noah gave a cheer, though I thought it was for my benefit rather than the band's.

We both listened to the music for a while—they weren't bad, though the singer sounded a little pitchy to me—then, made bold by cider and Noah's smile, I said, "I sing."

"Do you?" He grinned at me, genuinely interested.

"Yeah. Well, karaoke."

Noah leaned forward, his elbows on the table. "You any good?"

I shrugged. "I think so. I'm not bad anyway."

"I'd love to hear you sing." Noah flashed me a smile before lifting his glass to his lips. When a group of young women got up to dance, laughing drunkenly and whooping, Noah put his glass down and grabbed my hand. "Come on, let's go and dance!"

"I don't really think—" Noah was on his feet now, tugging my hand. I sighed and stood up. "I don't really think there's much room for dancing," I said. "And I'm definitely not drunk enough."

"Well, I'm stone-cold sober and I'm gonna dance." He let go of me, turned to the women—who only seemed too happy for him to join them—and raised his hands above his head. I stood on the outskirts, a bemused half smile on my face as Noah swayed his hips and clapped his hands. One of the women put her arm around Noah's waist, and he laughed and dropped an arm around her shoulders, before turning to beckon me to join them.

Rolling my eyes and thinking *what the hell*, I grabbed Noah's hip and latched myself into the circle of dancing women. We clung to one another, Noah and the women and me, and danced awkwardly and not entirely in rhythm in the small space in front of the band.

When the song stopped, we clapped and cheered and my head spun with giddiness though I'd only drunk one pint.

Noah turned to me, laughing and breathless, and said, "Good that, wasn't it?"

Our gazes met, and I had the biggest urge to kiss him. I cleared my throat. "Yeah, good fun." I put a hand on the small of his back and guided him back to our table.

I stopped in my tracks when I spotted Emmett in my chair. "Don't get attached," he warned me. "The boy is taken."

"You all right?" Noah asked. "Look like you've seen a ghost." He flopped down in his seat and sipped his lemonade. "Urgh, it's gone all warm."

"Uh huh." I blinked hard, but Emmett didn't disappear. "I'll get you a new one." I turned to the bar before Noah could question my reaction and glowered as Emmett joined me. "Can't you give me some privacy?"

"Absolutely not," Emmett said. "I'm here to stop you doing something stupid. He is engaged."

"I know that." I said it through clenched teeth, which I somehow managed to turn into a smile when the barman caught my eye. "Just a lemonade please, mate." I fished in my back pocket for my wallet.

I took the drink back to the table and passed it to Noah. He smiled at me. "Looks like you was talking to yourself just then," he said.

"Probably was," I agreed, taking my seat. "Bit of a mutterer."

Noah laughed. He drummed his fingers on the table, sipped his lemonade, and then asked, "So, how long've you worked for the Scrantons then? That manor's dead posh, innit?"

"As long as they've owned the place," I said. "I used to work for the previous owners. The Harpers." I stared at the table and picked at a knot in the wood.

"Nah, don't know 'em," Noah said.

My gaze turned to the bar, but Emmett had gone. "You didn't read the local papers then?" I asked. "There was a big explosion. Gas. The Scrantons had quite a lot of money knocked off because of all the damage."

There was a big cheer from the group of ladies at the other table, laughter, and a gaggle of voices as they all tried to speak over one another as well as the music. Noah was grinning as he watched them, and once again, his infectious smile cheered me.

He turned back to me. "Don't really read papers," he said. "Can't be doing with all the doom and gloom. Tony's always watching the news on telly. It drives me mad."

I tried not to look put out at the mention of his partner. "Does Tony work?" I asked. I didn't care, particularly, but I had to pretend I was interested.

"Yeah, he's working tonight, remember?" Noah said. "That's why he couldn't be here. He's a project manager at a construction company. It's right boring."

"Oh." Tony's job was boring. I was hoping Tony was boring too. I finished my cider.

Noah watched me with an impish grin on his face. Then he leaned forwards and said, "What do you do for fun around here? Is this it?"

I looked around at the band. "Pretty much. Not much of a 'scene' here."

"What do *you* do for fun? Besides karaoke."

"Uh…" God, I had to think of something that made me sound more exciting than Tony. "Karting," I said, pleased I'd remembered there was a track nearby. I'd been once, years ago, at my mate Freddie's 25th birthday bash. "I go go-karting." It was probably because it began with K, the same as karaoke. I was such a bloody idiot. I offered Noah a grin anyway.

"Sounds good," he said. "Can I come with you next time you go?"

"If you like."

"Really? What about this weekend?"

I raised my eyebrows. "Don't you want to spend the weekend with your feller?"

He wanted to spend the weekend with *me*. My heart palpitated so I sipped my drink to attempt an air of nonchalance.

"Can he come too?"

"Uh…"

Luckily, the lead singer gave a shout out for requests, and I took the opportunity, while I was pretending to be distracted by this, to think of an excuse to dump Tony. There wasn't enough room in my car for Noah *and* Tony, or they didn't allow groups of more than two people or didn't allow people called Tony.

Failing miserably, I said, "Sure."

Noah rewarded me with a grin. "Cool."

We spent the rest of the evening dancing and laughing and, I was pretty sure, flirting.

Chapter Six

A ROW OF glorious purple dahlias grew along the border right in front of the manor, the colour of them stunning against the yellow brick. They were top-heavy now and needed support, so I was busy staking them in place when a car pulled up in the driveway. I glanced back quickly and then again when I realised it was Joe Scranton.

He closed the car door, looked at me briefly, and then towards the manor. Persephone was a very lucky young woman, I had to admit. Joe wore khaki shorts and a T-shirt that clung to him enough for me to tell he had a six-pack under there. It took me a moment to realise the woman who emerged from the passenger side wasn't Persephone.

"Bleedin' 'ell, Joe!" she said. "This place is a bit posh, innit!" Her skirt was very short and her heels very high. I pulled my gaze back to the dahlias, telling myself she was his cousin or... just a friend. Whatever she was, it was none of my business.

I pushed a stake into the earth and knotted twine around the plant's stem. From the corner of my eye, I noticed Joe shepherding the woman inside, his hand low on her back.

Emmett appeared when I turned to reach for another stake, making me jump out of my skin.

"Curious," he said.

"What is?"

"You know what. That man is supposed to be dating my daughter."

I rolled my eyes. "Two straight people can be just friends, you know. They're not all shagging."

"Oh, come on," Emmett said. "You're thinking it just as much as I am. Go and see what they're doing."

"No! I'm working." I dusted mud from my hands. "Anyway, I'm not allowed in there. And if they're shagging, they would've gone upstairs."

"Remember when we did it in the library on my old Chesterfield?"

I grinned. "Yeah. Leather sofa and bare skin—not good."

"So go and look in the library window!" Emmett said, flapping a hand at the side of the manor. "Go."

I was sure they wouldn't be in the library. They would've gone to a bedroom, though if they were having an affair, why would Joe have brought her to his brother's house? Still, I downed tools and slunk around the side of the building. My heart beating hard, I peered in the library window.

The room didn't look much different to when the Harpers lived there. It was still a library. In fact, the shelving was full of Emmett's books. I knew some of his things had been sold along with the house, but it felt strange seeing the room as if Emmett would walk in at any moment. I'd not really had a proper look since the Scrantons had taken over—peering in windows was not usually something I did. A gaudy leopard-print rug dominated the centre of the room. Lamps with zebra-print shades flanked the chesterfield sofa, and a golden cherub, complete with shiny naked arse, sat proud atop the coffee table.

Emmett leaned over my shoulder and whispered in my ear. "Absolutely no taste."

I grunted a reply. The library door opened, and Joe and the woman entered. I ducked down and then peeped up over the sill. They were talking, their voices muffled, and Joe beckoned the woman over to a drinks cabinet where he poured them both a glass of champagne.

"They're celebrating something," I whispered to Emmett.

"But what?" Emmett replied.

I had no idea and I couldn't even guess. Still, it seemed innocent enough.

Joe looked towards the window, and I dropped down, heart racing. I hoped he hadn't seen me. He couldn't have seen me or he would surely have shouted at me to bugger off. Maybe he was too polite. I crawled under the window and out of the way and then got to my feet and jogged back to the front of the manor.

"Is that it?" Emmett asked, strolling over to join me. "You gained absolutely no information whatsoever."

"It's none of my business," I said, grabbing a cane. "What goes on in the manor stays in the manor. I'm only interested in the garden."

"That's awfully dull," Emmett said. "You'd make a terrible spy."

I rolled my eyes though I was smiling. "Good thing I don't want to be a spy."

FOR THE REST of that week, I didn't see Joe or the mysterious woman again. Zara patrolled the garden on Thursday morning, her dogs trailing at her heels and a magazine in her hand, and when she spotted me deadheading, she marched over and tapped her perfectly manicured fingernail at a picture in the magazine.

"Can you do something like this, Al?" she asked me.

I pulled my gaze away from one of the dogs as it cocked its leg on my wheelbarrow, and looked at the picture of a garden full of topiary animals. "I might be able to," I said hesitantly.

"Oh good. I want two little dogs, like my two, either side of the path here, and then maybe an angel or something up by the driveway. What do you reckon?"

I wasn't quite sure how to be diplomatic about how awful it would look. So I lied. "Actually, you'd need a really nice laurel or privet for something like that, and we just don't have the right soil for those here."

"Oh, balls," Zara said. "Back to the drawing board." She called her dogs and headed away, studying the magazine.

I smiled to myself and carried on with my work.

It wasn't until Friday that I started getting the twist of nerves in my gut. The weekend had almost arrived, and I was to go go-karting with Noah. And Tony. I tried to forget Tony was going too but failed miserably. What if Tony was an arse? Or worse, what if Tony was a really nice guy? I'd text Noah a few times, initially to let him know I'd booked the track and then just because I wanted to hear from him. One day he'd texted me: *just dun a cocker* (I presumed that was a type of dog) *at this man's house, right, and he's got all this dead pornographic artwork all over! I almost died! LOL x*

And I stared at the kiss and wondered if he'd meant to put it there or if he'd just typed x out of habit. Maybe he'd not even meant to text me. I wrote back, *that's so funny! x* just to see what he'd respond.

He came back with, *Knew you'd find it funny x*

I didn't text again as I didn't want to push my luck, but there was something about that little exchange that made me smile.

When Saturday arrived, I kept myself occupied by first visiting old Mrs Harper and getting up to speed on the latest gossip on the Harper clan and then pottering about in my own garden until it was time to shower and change.

I'd laid five different T-shirts on my bed, had two shirts hanging on my wardrobe door, and three pairs of jeans draped over the back of a chair.

Emmett joined me. He wore a mustard-coloured waistcoat under a tweed jacket and had a silk cravat around his neck. "What does one wear at a karting event?" he asked.

"Nothing like you've got on," I said. "And you're not coming."

"Not even for moral support?"

"Definitely not." I picked up a cream V-neck T-shirt. "Is this too plain? It's too plain. A dress shirt's too formal though, right? I want smart casual."

Emmett sat himself in my chair, and I snatched up my jeans before he creased them. "You always look lovely," he said.

I smiled. "I would kiss you if I could. Okay, how about stonewashed jeans and the navy polo shirt. Oh god, is that too much blue?"

Emmett laughed, so I grabbed the pillow off my bed and threw it at him. He dodged it easily and gave me a wide smile. "Wear the red V-neck with the indigo jeans and those red canvas shoes you have."

"Red shoes, no knickers," I said distractedly as I laid the jeans and T-shirt together on the bed. My mother used to say that. I wasn't entirely sure what it meant.

"He will be *gagging* for you," Emmett said, stealing up behind me.

"That's not what I want to happen," I replied. "Okay, it is. But Tony's going. I want Noah to look at me and think I'm hotter than his fiancé. That's all." I picked up the red T-shirt. "I do look good in this one."

I looked at myself in the mirror with the shirt held up in front of me. I wondered what Noah would be wearing.

I'D AGREED TO meet Noah—and Tony—at the track in the end, and I'd just gotten out of my car in the car park when a silver BMW pulled up alongside me. Noah grinned and waved at me from the passenger window, and my gaze slid over to Tony, though I couldn't really tell too much of what he looked like under his shades.

Noah got out of the car as Tony stopped the engine. He wore a white T-shirt with thin navy stripes, and he looked bloody gorgeous. "Hiya," he said. "We're not late, are we? Oh, this is Tony. Tony, Alistair."

Tone-eh. That's how he pronounced it. God, I loved his accent.

"All right?" I said to Tony.

Tony gave the slightest nod of acknowledgement but said nothing. He lifted his shades and looked towards the building. He was a slim man, nowhere near as buff as Noah, but tall with an air of power about him—almost like how I'd imagine a hired assassin or something. His nose was straight and strong, and he had designer stubble covering his chin and cheeks. He lowered his shades and turned back to Noah and me. "We going in or what?"

"Sure," I said. Noah flashed me a smile, and I led the way towards the hangar. Chequered flags flew outside, and I could hear karts roaring around the track, though couldn't see them from this side of the building.

We crunched across the gravelled car park together, and Noah said, "Dead exciting this, innit?"

"You won't win," Tony said. "Drive like a right pansy."

I supposed he was joking, though it didn't strike me as a particularly supportive thing to say, but Noah just laughed and gave him a playful shove. "Yeah, all right, you won't be saying that when you're eating my dust!"

"So you're good at this, eh, Alistair?"

I looked at Tony and then away. "Pretty good," I lied. I just hoped I remembered how to do it.

Tony chuckled, suggesting he didn't believe me. Cheeky sod. I clenched my fists and forced my lips into a smile. We entered the hangar with me leading the way—luckily, I remembered where I was going—and I headed over to the reception desk to get us signed in. The lady informed us we'd be racing with two others and that somebody would be with us soon to give us our race suits, helmets, and gloves.

Noah rubbed his hands together in glee, the excitement written all over his face, and we didn't have to wait long before a man called us into the changing area. The other two drivers were already there—two women—and we all introduced ourselves before the official handed us our outfits.

"Balaclava?" Noah said, eyeing what he'd just been given with a look of disgust on his face. "I'm not a criminal."

"Hygiene reasons," our guide said. "People are breathing all over the insides of the helmets, it's better to be safe than pretty."

"Urgh, yeah, that's dead gross," Noah agreed, putting the balaclava on. "How do I look?"

I opened my mouth to answer, but Tony got in first with, "Suits you."

"Yeah?" Noah asked, his voice muffled.

Tony laughed.

"You look fine," I assured him. I put my suit and balaclava on, and we tried on different helmets until everything fit nice and snug. My biggest worry had been losing to Tony, but at this point, I was wondering what would happen if I *did* crash.

Somebody slapped me on the back as we headed down to the track, but I wasn't sure who it was. The man in charge gave us a quick safety talk, showed us how to work the karts—*Alistair already knows all this*, Noah had said—and then supervised as we drove the karts from the pit area and onto the track.

We lined up. I was on the end with Noah right by my side, and he gave me a double thumbs up. I was too busy getting over that when the lights changed and the other drivers sped away. Cursing, I shoved the kart into gear and put my foot down.

I took the first corner far too fast, and my heart palpitated as the wheels lifted. I was aware of the sound of my own breathing, and the suit, uncomfortably close and warm, stuck to my skin. The two women were in front of me and, by pure fluke, I managed to squeeze past one of them.

Tony led the track, with the other woman and Noah a short distance behind him. Noah took the next corner too wide and both the woman and I slipped past. Part of me wanted to glance back, to see if he looked upset or impressed. The other part of me, the larger part, wanted to chase Tony down.

Somebody clipped the back of my kart, but I sped up. The rev and squeal of the karts filled my ears, and I forgot about the discomfort of the suit. I managed to overtake the woman on the next straight piece of track and almost caught Tony when we reached the bend, but he took it cleaner and accelerated faster and was gone before I could catch him.

We passed the chequered line on the road indicating we'd already completed one lap. God, if I didn't beat him...

The karts bunched again at the next corner and somebody tried to get past me. Glancing over, I saw it was Noah and instinctively let up on the accelerator. One of the women behind bumped me, and I hit the edge of the track, swerved, and came to a halt facing the opposite direction.

I slapped the steering wheel in frustration. As I manoeuvred the kart across the track, something hit me. Hard.

I remember a jolt up my spine and I remember waking up with Tony peering at me, his helmet tucked under his arm. "What did you do that for?" he said to me. And I must've blacked out.

When I woke again, I was in hospital. There were a lot of confusing sounds, flashes of lights—people were talking at me, but I couldn't take it in—pain in my leg and a pinprick in my arm and I was gone again.

Chapter Seven

I'D BROKEN A bone in my leg. Or, to be more precise, *Tony* had broken a bone in my leg when he'd hit me. He'd been coming up to lap me when I just pulled out in front of him. So he said. Part of me thought he'd rammed me on purpose, but I couldn't think the worst of people. Okay, I could, but I shouldn't.

The doctor put my leg in a plaster cast and told me to attend a fracture clinic in a week's time. I wouldn't be able to work for *six weeks*. The thought of not working sent me into a cold sweat. What the hell would I do?

To start with, I struggled on at home until I realised I couldn't pay the bills with no money coming in and found it difficult to do simple tasks like cook for myself. So I moved back with my dad and rented my place out to a young lad who'd just taken a job at McKenna's farm. Things were less stressful but no less awkward. Dad and I still didn't know how to hold a conversation. He cooked our meals or drove us to the pub. I saw Emmett more often—to the point where Dad had caught me talking to him and I had to explain it was just a comfort thing, and I sometimes spoke to Mum too.

Noah visited while I still lived at my own place, and then once I moved into Dad's he'd texted me a few times and asked how I was getting on. Zara rang and popped round with a 'Get Well Soon' card and a bunch of flowers. She promised me my job was safe and that they'd just hired in one of David's mates—who, Zara said, was a bloody awful gardener—until I was ready to return to work.

I spent a lot of time in my bedroom. I didn't sing. I desperately wanted to fuck Noah. Instead, I masturbated while Emmett watched.

It was really. Bloody. Depressing.

I WOKE UP one day to my phone ringing. It was late afternoon and I, like the studmuffin I am, had a string of drool hanging from my mouth to my pillow. Fumbling for my phone, I wiped my lips, squinted at the name on the screen, and, surprised to see it was Noah, attempted to sound a little more awake as I answered.

"Hello?"

"Hiya! How are you?"

I rubbed my eyes, trying to wake myself up. Why was he ringing me? He never rang, only texted. "Okay. I guess."

"Cor, what's the matter with you? You sound dead grumpy."

"Just woke up," I mumbled.

"Oh. Soz. How's the leg?"

"Fine." I looked at the clock on my wall. Five in the afternoon. What did he want?

There was silence on the phone. Finally, Noah said, "Can I see you?"

That woke me up. I heaved myself into a sitting position and, catching sight of myself in the wardrobe mirror, tidied my hair with my fingers. Not that Noah could see me.

"If you want to," I said. "I mean, yeah, that'd be nice. Don't get much company."

"Me and Tony have had a row," Noah said. "Just need to get out of here for a bit."

"Oh." I scratched my face. I had a rough beard and desperately needed a shave. "You all right?"

"Yeah. Well... yeah, I guess so. He's just stressed, you know. With work. I just need to see a friendly face."

Maybe they were going to split up! No, I shouldn't think that. Didn't want to get my hopes up. "I can meet you somewhere," I said. "We can have a drink, have a laugh."

"Sounds good. Or... I could come to yours?"

I frowned. "My dad will probably be here—"

"I don't mind. I'd like to meet him. I don't want you to drag yourself out to come meet me, not with your leg and everything."

I smiled a little. "I'm not bed bound. How about you come and pick me up, and we'll go to the pub for a drink?" I suggested. "Then you can meet the old man when you take me home. If you still want to."

"Cool," Noah said. I could hear the smile in his voice. "See you later."

He hung up before I could ask what time. Smiling, I dragged myself out of bed to get ready.

NOAH KNOCKED ON the door, and I leaned on one crutch as I opened it. He flashed me the biggest grin as soon as he saw me, and I smiled. He'd changed his hair—that was the first thing I'd noticed—with shaved sides and a longer quiff on top.

"Like it?" he said, waving a hand at his head.

"Looks great." I hopped out onto the doorstep and turned to lock the door. The second thing I noticed, as I followed Noah down the path towards his van, was that his backside looked terrific in his grey cargo trousers.

He opened the van door for me, though he didn't have to, and closed it carefully behind me. When he got into the driver's seat, I asked, "You okay?"

"Fine," he said. "Oh, you mean the fight with Tony? Yeah. He's just got a right cob on 'cause I wanted to go out at the weekend and he didn't."

"He can stay home, can't he?" I asked. I noticed the van smelled of dogs and wondered if Noah remembered I was supposed to be allergic. I pondered faking a sneeze.

"He can, but he gets proper jealous sometimes," Noah said. "You know. If I'm out without him. He thinks every man wants me. Mind, he's probably right."

I laughed.

"What?" Noah asked, grinning over at me. "It's probably true! I bet you want me, don't you?"

"No." I was lying through my teeth, and I said it with a smile, but I think Noah believed me.

"Really?" he asked. "Aw, that's a shame; I think you're quite fit."

My heart beat a little faster, but I managed a shrug and said, "Pity you're engaged then."

Noah didn't reply because we'd completed the short trip to the pub. He pulled into the car park. As I opened the door and swung my legs out, awkwardly grappling with my crutches, I repeated Noah's words in my head. He thought I was fit!

Emmett appeared by the van door, making me fall back into my seat. "Quite fit," he said. "Quite. I'd be insulted, Alistair, if I were you."

Then Noah was there, peering into the van. "You all right? Need a hand?"

"Yeah," I said, letting him heave me out. "Thanks." Emmett had vanished, and I looked back over my shoulder as we headed towards the pub, willing him not to appear like that again.

I took a seat at a table in the corner of the room, next to the window and the unlit fireplace, while Noah went to the bar and ordered us drinks. I propped my crutches by my chair and stared out the window.

"You sure you're all right?" Noah asked when he returned with the drinks. He sat and placed a glass of juice in front of me. "You look miles away."

"I'm fine." I offered him a smile. "You should go out at the weekend, you know. If you want. Without Tony, I mean."

Noah shrugged. "Kinda wanted to go out with my man, you know? Doesn't matter though." He reached for his glass and took a sip. I watched his Adam's apple.

"What's up with your dad, then?" Noah asked.

I didn't understand what he meant, and I must've looked confused because he continued. "You sounded like you didn't want me at yours if your dad was home. He's not, you know, funny about gays, is he?"

I laughed. "No! Nothing like that. He's great about all that, always been supportive and everything, it's just...since Mum died, we don't really talk anymore. Not properly."

It was the first time I'd mentioned Mum to Noah, and I chanced looking up at him from my juice. He had a concerned frown, and when I met his gaze, he reached across the table to touch my hand briefly. "Go on."

I scratched the side of my face. "She died of cancer," I said. "Breast cancer. Couple of years ago now."

"I'm sorry," Noah said.

I cleared my throat and picked up my glass before taking a sip to dislodge the lump threatening to stick in my oesophagus.

"I haven't seen my dad since I was two," Noah said, and I looked at him in surprise. "One day he was there; the next he was gone, and I never saw him again. We moved away, me and Mum, and she met a new man. Chris. He's my step-dad now. Got a little sister too—half sister—told you about Dani, didn't I?"

"Yeah... Johnny Hammers?"

Noah grinned. "That's it. She's dead good. We should go to one of her shows."

"She has her own show now?"

"Up in Bristol. Tony won't come. He thinks it's daft. But we should go, you and me."

"I'd love to." I met Noah's gaze again and held it until we both looked away in awkward silence.

I drank more juice and looked out the window again as a cat strolled nonchalantly across the road.

"Hey," Noah said, "so I was at this man's house, right, with the cocker I told you about..."

The awkwardness passed, and I listened to Noah's story with a smile.

MY DAD HAD parked his van in the drive so I knew he was home. I leaned on a crutch as I unlocked the door, and when I looked anxiously at Noah, he gave me a thumbs up. I sighed and headed into the house.

"Dad?" I called.

There was no answer. I led Noah inside. He closed the door for me as I hopped down the hallway towards the kitchen.

"Tea?" I asked. "Coffee?"

"Coffee, ta," Noah said. "This is nice. The house. Is this where you grew up?"

"Uh huh." I put the kettle on to boil and then turned and nodded at the notches in the doorframe. "See that? That's me growing up."

"Oh yeah, one of those height things!" Noah said, touching the marks. "Aw! That's dead cute, that is."

I chuckled. "Right."

"Well, I didn't have nothing like that," Noah said. He sounded a little sad, but I didn't have time to say anything to cheer him up as my dad wandered down the hall and stopped in the doorway.

"Didn't know we had visitors," he said.

"Dad, this is Noah," I said. "Works up at the manor with Mrs Scranton's dogs."

"Oh ah," Dad said.

He and Noah eyed each other warily until Noah offered his hand and said, "Nice to meet you. Al's told me all about you."

"Doubt it," Dad replied. He shook Noah's hand.

The awkwardness was already making me want the ground to open up beneath me. I turned back to the kettle, willing it to boil. "Drink, Dad?"

"Ah, go on then." He sat himself at the kitchen table, and to my surprise, Noah joined him.

"Al was just showing me those marks," Noah explained.

"His mother did those," Dad said. "Every year, she'd make him go and stand against the frame and she'd cut another notch."

I said nothing. I listened with my back to them both, heart thumping painfully. My dad was having a *conversation*. The kettle clicked, and I poured the water.

"You can see where he had a growth spurt and everything," Noah said.

"Took a while for it to kick in, though. Proper little weed, he was, for a time."

"Not a weed no more, though, is he?"

I pretended not to hear, stirring the coffee as loudly as I could manage.

"Good-looking lad he is now," my dad said, a hint of pride in his voice. "Just like his old man. Isn't that right, Al?"

I turned with a mug in hand, and Noah leapt up to get the other two. My face was hot and I hoped I wasn't blushing.

"All right, Dad," I said, laughing a little. I passed him his drink, and as I turned to take mine from Noah, our hands touched.

Our gazes met. Noah let go and cleared his throat. Behind me, Dad got up from his chair. "I'll take mine upstairs, let you two lads chat. Nice meeting you, Noah."

"You too, Mr…" A look of horror passed over Noah's face, and when he looked at me, I couldn't help but laugh.

"Ellis!" I said.

"Mr Ellis," Noah said quickly. "Oh god, I'm so sorry. I didn't know Al's surname!"

I was still laughing. Dad looked from Noah to me and back again. He slapped Noah on the shoulder and headed out of the room.

Noah chuckled. "Bet he thinks I'm a right dickhead."

"No, he doesn't," I said, sitting down. "He likes you."

"Yeah?"

I nodded.

"Do you like me?" Noah asked, sitting in the chair beside me. He hugged his coffee in his hands.

"'Course I do."

"No, I mean... *like* me like me."

I looked at Noah, gazed into those dark eyes. He leaned forwards suddenly and kissed me and, surprised, I kissed him back. His lips were full and very soft, and I slipped my tongue into his mouth.

As fast as he'd moved to kiss me, he pulled back. "Oh god, I'm sorry," he muttered, pushing his chair back. "I shouldn't have done that. I better go. I'm really sorry."

He headed out of the room while I snatched at my crutches. "Noah!" I called. "Wait a minute!" But I heard the front door close before I could even get out of my seat.

Chapter Eight

I'D JUST COME back from having physio at the hospital and asked the taxi driver to drop me off in the village so I could pay old Mrs Harper a visit. I leaned on one crutch as I fished notes from my wallet to pay the driver, giving him a tip as he'd helped me in and out of the car without making it seem a chore. Then, I waited for him to drive away before crossing the road.

Old Mrs Harper's gate was shut, and I cursed beneath my breath. Leaning awkwardly, I reached for the handle and ended up dropping a crutch. I cursed again, louder this time, and Emmett, behind me, said, "Language!"

Only when I turned to complain about the bloody crutches, I saw it wasn't Emmett at all but a young man with a mop of blond hair and slate-grey eyes. I blinked at him.

"What *are* you doing?" he asked, picking my crutch up for me and handing it back.

"Thanks. Trying to open the gate." I'd thought it was obvious.

"Do you know my grandmother?" he asked, opening the gate.

"Your grandmother?" My mind raced. Emmett had no sons, only daughters. No wait, his brother had a son. Only they lived in Scotland or somewhere.

"Yes." The man laughed. "Are you at the wrong house? Poor chap, you seem quite confused."

"No, I know Mrs Harper," I said. "Used to work for her and the late Mr Harper."

"Uncle Emmett?" He headed down the path towards the door and knocked before looking back at me with interest. His face was young but handsome, and I could see no resemblance to Emmett at all. "Doing what?"

"Gardener," I said. "Still work at the manor."

"Good for you."

It was my turn to smile. He'd sounded patronising, though I was positive he hadn't meant it that way. Old Mrs Harper opened the door and squinted at her grandson.

"Arthur. Good. I was expecting you weeks ago."

Arthur leaned down and kissed his grandmother on the cheek before moving past her into the cottage, calling, "Sorry, Granny, busy busy!"

Old Mrs Harper turned back to me. I said, "Sorry, I didn't know you'd have company. I'll come back."

"Don't be silly," she said, beckoning me in. "I can't turn you away, you're practically a cripple. Come in. Arthur? Put the kettle on."

Arthur smiled at me as he passed us in the hall on the way to the kitchen, and I followed his grandmother into the lounge.

"You can't use that word," I said, sitting down. "Anyway, I reckon I'll be back to work in no time. And I'll be able to pick you up some more bits and pieces soon."

She waved a hand at me and sat in the armchair. "Arthur will do all that now. His father sent him down here to look after me, seeing as my beloved granddaughters are next to useless."

"How are they all?" I propped my crutches carefully beside the sofa so nobody would trip over them.

"Isabelle had the baby. Oh, what have they called her?" She scrunched up her face, trying to remember. "Something silly. Xanthe, that was it. Poor little thing."

"It's unusual," I said.

"Very diplomatic, Alistair. Anyway, so she's busy, fair enough. The twins are on a skiing holiday—one of them's bound to end up in your condition, I shouldn't wonder—Harriet's still moaning about the sale. Oh, and she's trying to contest the will now, too, but I shan't go into that. And Persephone..."

"Still seeing Joe Scranton?"

"Exactly. Awful man."

At that moment, Arthur came back into the room with a tea tray, which he placed on the coffee table. He'd made it the proper way—that is, he'd set out a china teapot, teacups and saucers, and included a sugar bowl complete with little silver spoon. He poured a cup for his grandmother and then looked set to do the same for me when I put out my hand to stop him.

"I can do it," I said. "Thank you."

"Of course," he said, hitching up his trousers to sit beside me. "No offense meant."

"None taken." I made my tea and lifted the cup to my lips, aware both Arthur and old Mrs Harper were watching me and suddenly feeling very large and clumsy.

I sipped my tea and smiled at them both.

"So, you're a gardener. That must be terribly interesting," Arthur said, at which, old Mrs Harper snorted.

"Uh...yeah. I guess. I mean, I find it interesting."

"Of course, you wouldn't do it otherwise."

"No, I guess not," I agreed.

"And your new bosses, are they nice?" Arthur asked. "Have they made many changes at the manor?"

Old Mrs Harper put her teacup back onto the saucer with a clink. "Don't interrogate the poor boy," she said. "Let him drink his tea."

Arthur offered me an apologetic smile and turned his attention back to his grandmother instead. I listened to their conversation, nodded whenever they involved me, and finished my drink. When I reached for my crutches, Arthur leapt to his feet.

"Are you off?" he asked. "Do you need help at all? Let me get the door for you."

I laughed at his eagerness to help—or get rid of me—and noticed his grandmother roll her eyes as I pulled myself up. "He reminds me of a spaniel I used to have," she said to me. "An absolute darling but ultimately a pain in the arse."

"Charming, Granny," Arthur said, opening the door for me.

I just laughed politely and made my way around the coffee table towards the door. "Thanks for the tea, Mrs Harper," I said. "Give me a call if you need anything."

I hobbled out into the hallway and to the front door with Arthur behind me. "Are you all right? Do you need a hand getting home?"

"That's very kind of you," I said, turning back to look at him on the doorstep. "But I'll just call a taxi. I'll be fine."

"Nonsense! I've got my car; I'll give you a lift. Wait right there. I'll fetch my keys."

He disappeared before I could say anything, and I waited for him, though I was annoyed he hadn't listened. He touched my arm as he passed me and made his way down the pathway and off down the road where I now noticed a silver Audi.

"I can walk that far," I muttered.

Arthur had to turn his car around and then drive all of twenty feet before he stopped outside the cottage. I just stood on old Mrs Harper's doorstep like an idiot as Arthur got out the car and jogged back down the pathway to me. I must've been scowling because his smile dropped when he reached me.

"Not an Audi fan?" he asked.

"No, I just...the taxi would've been fine."

"Oh. Well, I'm here now. Come on."

We walked to the car together, and I let Arthur take my crutches to put them in the back. The car smelled new, and I eyed the spotless interior wondering how long he'd had it. Arthur got into the driver side and turned on the engine.

"Directions?" he asked.

I gave him directions to my dad's house and replied politely to Arthur's questioning on the drive there. I knew he was after something, but it wasn't until we pulled up in my dad's driveway and Arthur put his hand on my leg that I worked out what.

I cleared my throat. "If I could just get my crutches..."

"You are *sexy*," Arthur said, his hand sliding farther towards my groin. "My father said Uncle had a gay gardener. You were part of the gossip after Auntie ran off. Nobody mentioned you were hot."

"Um. Thank you." My breath caught in my throat, and I pushed his hand away. "I should get inside."

"Your father doesn't appear to be in," Arthur said. "You told me he might be at work still. Can't I come in?"

I stared at him. He had a wicked look in his blue eyes.

"I want you, Alistair," he said. "Right now."

His confidence turned me on immediately, and I nodded and reached for my crutches. Arthur got them for me and hurried round the car to pass them to me.

"Keys," he said, and I handed him my house keys without any argument. He reached the front door before me and unlocked it, practically dragging me inside with him when I joined him.

We were kissing before the door had even closed, and Arthur was soon reaching into my pants. "Upstairs," I said breathlessly, pushing him away.

He allowed me to go first, clearly not sure where he was going, and I took the stairs as fast as I could manage with the crutches and threw the bloody things down when I reached my bed. Arthur closed my door and looked me up and down.

"I can do all the work," he said. "You just lie back."

AFTERWARDS, WE BOTH lay in silence. Arthur stared at the ceiling, his blond hair slick to his forehead. I couldn't take my eyes off Emmett, who stood by the window with his arms folded, gazing out to the street.

"I can't believe you just fucked my nephew," he said, not turning to me.

I didn't reply. I didn't want Arthur to think I was nuts. Instead, I pulled my gaze away and looked at Arthur. "All right?" I asked.

"Father doesn't know I'm gay," he replied. "And neither does Granny, so you mustn't say anything."

"I don't think it'll come up in conversation; don't worry. I don't think old Mrs Harper would be bothered though."

"I don't want my father knowing," Arthur said again.

It wasn't any of my business, so I nodded. Arthur moved over to me and nuzzled against my chest so I put an arm around him, even though Emmett still stood in the room. Whatever was outside must have been fascinating because he didn't turn to look at me at all. I wished he was in my arms suddenly and a pang of loss hit me.

Arthur traced his finger around my nipple, and I took hold of his hand to make him stop. "We should get up," I said, gently. "My dad'll be back soon."

"No time for another round?"

"My leg's sore. I think you'll break me if we go again." My leg was fine, but I was no longer in the mood. The room felt oppressive and Emmett's presence bothered me.

Arthur heaved a dramatic sigh and got up. "Granny will be missing me," he said. He reached for his clothes, and I watched him get dressed. "Can I see you again?"

"Yeah," I said as Emmett's gaze finally met mine. "I'd like that."

Chapter Nine

ARTHUR AND I met sporadically after our initial tryst. We found it difficult to coincide when he was free from old Mrs Harper and I was alone at Dad's. When we did get a chance to be together, it was just for sex, and I soon found myself closing my eyes to avoid having to look at Emmett. We would text each other, but every time my phone buzzed, I snatched at it, hoping it was Noah.

It never was.

A week before my cast was due for removal, I took a taxi to Whitecott Manor. It rained and wet leaves smacked into the windscreen as we drove up the driveway. I frowned at how many of the bloody things had gathered on the lawn and wondered why the temporary gardener wasn't out there raking them up. The driver handed me my crutches as I got out of his taxi, and I asked him to wait while I hurried to the door.

The Scrantons' blue sports car was parked in the drive so I knew they were home, though it took two rings of the bell before even the dogs noticed. I winced as they yapped and barked, hoping Zara would grab them hold before they could go for me.

It was Mr Scranton who opened the door. He didn't stop the dogs and they ran past him to jump up at me, hopping on their back feet, barking, while I froze up.

"Zara, will you get these bloody dogs in!" David yelled.

I gripped my crutches tight. Zara called and the dogs ran back inside, their claws skittering across the flooring. David Scranton glowered at me. "Not back at work then?" he asked.

"That's what I'm here for," I said. "To let you know I can start next week."

He grunted. Then yelled, "It's the gardener!"

He glowered at me some more and then walked away when Zara appeared, carrying one of the little dogs. "Al!" she exclaimed, leaning forward to kiss both my cheeks. "We haven't half missed you. Look at the bloody state of my lawn!"

"I did notice," I said. "I'll be back next week. The cast's coming off and everything'll get back to normal."

"Oh, that is good," Zara said. "Why don't you come in for a cuppa?"

The taxi still waited behind me, and I turned to wave a hand at it, glad of an excuse not to go inside with the dogs. "Driver's waiting."

"Send him on," Zara said. "David'll give you a lift home."

"No, no, I..."

As I looked back at the taxi again, another vehicle pulled into the driveway. A white van. Noah's van.

"Bloody hell, I forgot the groomer was coming. Sorry, Al"

"No worries," I said. "I'll head on. I'll see you next week."

Zara was barely paying me attention now. She waved up at Noah as he got out of the van, and called, "I'll go and find Coco, Noah. I'll leave the door open!" She patted me on the arm and then disappeared back inside.

I stood on the doorstep like an idiot until my brain engaged properly and I headed towards the taxi. As Noah and I passed, he stopped and said, "You're looking better. More colour in you, I mean."

I turned back to him. "Thanks."

We both stood in silence. The rain had eased to a light drizzle, not quite enough to use as an excuse to move on.

"So...you back at work then?" Noah asked.

"Next week."

Noah nodded. "Right. Well. I better..." He jerked a thumb towards the manor.

"Yeah," I agreed. I turned away, but Noah spoke again.

"I'm sorry I haven't texted or nothing. It's just, you know." I decided to stay quiet. Noah took a step closer to me. "And I'm sorry, you know? For..." He glanced back over his shoulder before he whispered. "—*kissing you*. If we could just...forget about it."

"Already forgotten," I said. "I'm seeing someone actually." I don't really know why I said it. A part of me hoped he was jealous.

"Oh!" He sounded surprised. "Right. Well, that's good. What's his name?"

"Arthur."

"Oh. My granddad was called Arthur."

I laughed at that, and Noah grinned. "Hey," he said. "We should get together sometime. You and Arthur and me and Tony. It'll be fun."

I wanted to get back to the taxi now. I was sure the driver would beep his horn at me at any moment and lying to Noah made me uncomfortable. "He's not really into the whole 'couples' thing," I said.

"Really?" Noah said, the disbelief evident in his voice. "Does he exist, this Arthur?"

"Yes, of course he does!"

"All right, I believe you! Get him to come out with us then. This Sunday. We'll go out in Yeovil."

"Okay," I agreed. "I won't be able to do much dancing with my leg like this, mind. And I'm not sure Arthur will agree to come anyway, so don't get your hopes up."

"I'll see you both Sunday," Noah said, grinning at me. "I'll text you."

He walked towards the manor, and I headed back to the taxi, smiling to myself.

I OPENED MY mouth and let out a low moan. I kept my eyes closed, because if I looked at Arthur with his lips around my cock, I'd see Emmett standing just behind him with a look of disapproval on his face.

"What...what are you doing this Sunday?" I thought to ask him while he was distracted, catch him off guard. I twisted my fist into my duvet.

Arthur stopped for long enough to say, "Why?"

"I just—" I had to stop to mutter a curse. Arthur was particularly good with his tongue. He laughed at my response, his chuckle vibrating through me and making me squirm.

I opened my eyes to look at him. "We've been invited out on Sunday."

"We?" He shifted up the bed so he was closer to my face and pumped my cock with his fist instead.

I nodded, swallowed, and closed my eyes again. "A double date thing. Friend invited me."

"Hm." Arthur moved back down the bed and once more the glorious warmth of his mouth wrapped around me. He quickly brought me to climax, and I was still twitching when he said, "I'll come."

"You will? To the date thing?"

He laughed and straddled me. He was naked and erect, and I gazed at his cock, aware Emmett sat by the window, filing his nails.

"To the date thing," he agreed. "It'll be nice to meet your friends. I'd like to come now, too. You can't leave me wanting."

"No," I agreed, grinning. "Though you do look hot like that."

I ignored Emmett's snort of derision and concentrated on Arthur, though my mind wandered to Noah.

ARTHUR'S CAR WAS so pristine I was almost scared to touch anything on our journey to Yeovil to meet Noah and Tony. I was tense, though whether from trying to keep my hands in my lap and feet off the mat or thinking about Noah I wasn't quite sure. Arthur didn't know where he was going so I had to direct him, but we soon parked up in the cinema car park, ready to walk into town.

"Are you sure you don't mind not drinking?" I asked as Arthur handed my crutches over. "We could've got a taxi."

"I don't mind," Arthur said. "I shouldn't get drunk anyway. I've promised Granny I'll take her shopping tomorrow, and I can't do that with a hangover."

I nodded. It was a chilly evening, but I still saw plenty of people out wearing next to nothing. We walked past the cinema and the bowling alley and the Italian restaurant with its fifties music leaking out into the street, and headed on up into town. Litter blew across the pavement in front of me, tangling briefly with one of my crutches. When I looked up, I spotted Noah outside the bar where we'd agreed to meet and he flashed me a grin when he noticed me.

"Hiya!" he called, joining us. He wore a blue T-shirt despite the fact he was shivering, and I couldn't help but notice the goose pimples on his arms. He held out his hand to Arthur.

"Arthur, Noah, Noah, Arthur," I said as the two men shook hands. Arthur stood taller, I realised, though not by much.

"Where's Tony?" I asked. Hoping, of course, that he hadn't made it.

"Inside propping up the bar," Noah replied. "We going in or what? I'm freezing my tits off."

We followed him in, the warmth hitting us immediately. Lots of people milled about, and I knocked a few legs with my crutches as we squeezed to the bar. I noticed the microphone in the corner of the room and, realising I'd seen it, Noah nudged my arm and said, "Karaoke later."

"Do you sing, Noah?" Arthur asked.

"Al does."

Arthur looked at me in surprise. "Are you any good?"

"You might find out later," I said. I gave Tony a polite nod when we reached him and allowed Noah to introduce him to Arthur. I noticed the way his gaze travelled down Arthur's torso and I bristled. As soon as I had space, I propped up my crutches and hooked an arm around Arthur's waist.

"I'll get the drinks in," Arthur said. "What's everybody having?"

As we gave him our orders, Tony and I eyed each other warily—him looking away first with a smirk on his lips. I wanted him to know I knew he'd done this to me. My broken leg was his fault.

With our drinks in hand (Arthur carrying mine for me), Noah ploughed through the people to a booth and we followed after him. The seats were soft and plush—a stark contrast to the clear-glass table, and when we sat down, Tony immediately threw his arm around Noah's shoulders, as if he owned him. I resisted the urge to do the same to Arthur, though I smiled when he gave my thigh a squeeze under the table.

"Alistair's back at work soon," Noah told Tony.

"Oh yeah," Tony said. "How's the leg?"

"Getting better." I tried not to say it through gritted teeth.

"You groom the dogs at the manor, Noah?" Arthur asked. "How do you find the new owners?"

I lifted my pint to my lips and forced myself to stop glowering at Tony.

"Yeah, dead nice," Noah said. "Well, I only speak to Zara really, but she's nice."

"My family used to own the place," Arthur said.

"Oh right, you're a Harper?"

"He's the nephew of my old boss," I explained to Noah.

"You sound posh," Tony said, leaning back in his seat. He wore a leather jacket, and I thought he could've offered it to Noah when he'd been waiting outside for us. "You didn't want to buy the place?"

Arthur laughed a little, clearly embarrassed. "Well, I live in Scotland with my father so..."

"So you're not staying down here then?"

"Leave 'im alone, Tony," Noah said, reaching for his drink.

"I'm only asking!"

"He's looking after his grandmother," I explained. "And I'm taking full advantage of him being here." I leaned over and kissed Arthur on the cheek, mentally telling Tony to piss off.

We sipped our drinks and made idle chitchat for a while. Then, a guy approached the microphone and announced karaoke was about to start and we'd better sign up if we wanted a go. Noah grinned at me immediately.

"Go on then!" he said.

I played it modest, but I was itching to get up there and show off. "I don't know what I should sing," I said.

"Something by Madonna," Arthur said, nudging me.

Tony laughed. I gave Arthur a 'cute, but no' look and gripped my crutches to heave myself from my seat. As I squeezed through the throng of people, the first drumbeats of Joan Jett's *I love Rock and Roll* kicked in and an already-drunk-looking young man stepped up to play air guitar with the microphone.

I reached the woman with the clipboard by one of the speakers and pointed to a track on her list and scribbled down my name. Everybody in the bar was singing now and a familiar flutter of excitement stirred in my guts.

I turned to make my way back to my table, but stopped when Emmett appeared in front of me. He wore red leather, just like Joan Jett in her music video, and I blurted out a laugh.

"Don't you like it?" he asked, spreading his arms.

"Yeah, you look very fetching," I said, sidling past him. "Go away."

"Oh come on, Alistair! You know I love hearing you sing!"

I sat next to Arthur again and picked up my drink. "Isn't anybody else having a go?" I asked.

"God no, I sound like a drowned cat," Arthur said. "I wouldn't want to subject you to that."

"Tony, can we have a go?" Noah asked, giving his fiancé a pleading look I would've found impossible to refuse.

Tony just laughed. "No! I'm not making myself look like a prat up there."

"Aw, go on. It's only a bit of fun."

"I said no."

Noah sat back in his seat, dejected. When his gaze met mine, I offered him a smile and said, "Why don't you come up with me?"

"Can I?" He perked up again and looked at Tony for permission.

"If you want to make yourself look like an idiot, go for it," Tony said with a shrug.

"We'll look like idiots together," I said.

"Why's it called Karaoke anyway?" Noah asked. "Isn't that, like, something to do with suicide?"

I had no idea what he meant and looking at the frown on Arthur's face made me realise I wasn't the only one. Tony laughed though and, reaching for his drink, said, "That's kamikaze." He chuckled some more. "Good thing he's got a pretty face, eh?"

"All right. I don't speak Japanese, do I?" Noah said. He didn't seem too put out by Tony's comment, though personally I was itching to give Tony a smack.

I looked over at the microphone as a woman took the stage and encouraged the audience to clap and cheer. A few people obliged. Most seemed more interested in their drinks. The first beats of 'Girls Just Want to Have Fun' kicked in.

"I love Cyndi Lauper, me," Noah said.

I smiled. Tony looked bored. The woman's voice wasn't half bad—she was much better than the previous guy—and she had stage presence too. I found myself watching her, so much so that Arthur had to give my arm a little shake to get my attention.

"Can I squeeze by?" he asked. "Bathroom break."

I got up and let him pass. Tony excused himself and got up too, following after Arthur to the toilets. When I sat back down, I reached across the table to touch Noah's hand.

"Everything okay with you and Tony?" I asked.

"What?" He turned from watching the woman. "Oh yeah. He's always grumpy like that. It's all right. Hey, your Arthur's a bit of all right, isn't he, eh? You've done good there."

I laughed. "Thanks! Yeah, he's a good bloke."

Noah nodded. We gazed at each other until it became awkward and instinctively we both reached for our drinks.

"When are we on?" Noah asked.

"Next."

We fell silent again. I vaguely wondered what was taking Arthur so long in the bathroom, and when I spotted him coming back through the crowd, I greeted him a little too enthusiastically, and Noah, spotting Tony behind Arthur, did likewise.

"We're up," I told Arthur, taking my crutches. "Be prepared to be dazzled."

Arthur chuckled. "I'm looking forward to it."

Noah and I headed to the microphone, Noah leaning close to me to say, "I'm a bit nervous now."

"You'll be fine!"

"I don't even know what we're singing."

We stood in front of the microphone, so close to each other our hips touched. I held my crutches tight, my palms weirdly sweaty. The room smelled of alcohol and ladies perfume, and everything closed in on me in a way that hadn't happened since the very first time I'd sang in public.

Somebody whistled. Arthur, I realised, and I flashed him a smile.

"The Strokes," I said to Noah. "Last Nite."

"I know that one."

The relief in his voice made me grin, and I pointed at the karaoke machine. "Get ready."

Guitars strummed and then the drums kicked in and Noah, startled, laughed a little when I began singing before he grabbed the microphone with me and joined in. I tried to focus on the words, though I knew them, and not on Noah standing so very close to me. Every time our eyes met we both laughed like school boys, so it wasn't the best I'd ever performed, but I had the most fun. I didn't want the song to end but when it did—and we received a round of applause and a few whistles—I had to remind myself I was there with Arthur. Arthur, who gave me a kiss when I returned to my seat, and not Noah, who didn't get so much as a peck from Tony.

Chapter Ten

I MOVED BACK home and returned to work the next week, though unfortunately the Scrantons had decided to keep on the temporary gardener, Ray, in case I needed help. I didn't. And I didn't like Ray either. He was a sour-faced older gentleman, with a flat cap and pot belly. Sometimes he worked with a cigarette hanging out his mouth and other times I'd catch him smirking at me for no apparent reason.

It was early October, and the trees around the edge of the estate were dropping their leaves. I raked, regularly, and added the leaves to one of the compost heaps to make leaf mould. Ray, however, seemed to assign himself the easy jobs and I often found him in the potting shed—*my* potting shed—flicking through a magazine and claiming he was ordering in seeds for next year.

"I should tell Zara you want him gone," Emmett told me, as I drove my spade through a crown of rhubarb to divide it up. "Otherwise you'll be stuck with him, and he makes the place look untidy."

"I might do," I said. "I just need to catch her when she's not busy."

"I'm sure he's up to something."

"He's not up to anything. That's the problem." I hefted half the rhubarb into the wheelbarrow so I could transplant it elsewhere.

"I saw him peering in the library window earlier."

I'd seen him too, and I'd almost asked him what the hell he was doing, but it'd not been so long ago that I'd been doing just the same with Emmett. "He's just being nosey."

"He could be on the rob!" Emmett sounded so indignant that I laughed. "I'm serious. You need to watch him, my dear. Catch him in the act."

"Hmm," I said. "I'll keep an eye on him."

LATER, JUST AS the light was beginning to fail and I was chucking some tools in the back of my car, I noticed Ray hanging around the back of the manor house. I left my car and headed down to him—Ray and myself didn't park on the driveway, but pulled up in a lane behind the house so we weren't in the way—to find out what he was doing.

"I'm heading home," I called to him as I drew nearer. I noticed how he startled at my voice, as if I'd caught him doing something he shouldn't.

He clutched his dirty cap in his hands, and he put it back on his head when I reached him. "Right y'are," he said. "Catch 'ee tomorrow."

I paused. Then, curiosity got the better of me and I said, "What *are* you doing?"

"Oh. This 'n' that. You know."

I didn't know. My brows knit together. Realising I wasn't just going to leave him to it, Ray said, "Mrs Scranton wanted me to stay on a bit and help her pick out some roses for next year."

"Zara's gone out," I said. "She takes the dogs to a class on a Monday."

"Ah, I know, I know. I'm waiting for her to come back. You head on, lad, don't mind me."

"Wouldn't it be best to just...talk to her tomorrow?"

"You just go 'ome and don't worry about what I'm doing." He was agitated now, his face red. He shifted from one foot to the other and I noticed he'd clenched his fists.

Emmett walked up behind me and peered close at Ray.

"He's hiding something," he said. "Go back to your car and wait to see what he does. We don't want to scare him off."

I nodded. "All right. See you tomorrow then."

"Ah, cheers, then."

I frowned again but left him to it, making my way across the lawn to the little iron gate that led out into the lane. I sat in my car, wondering what the hell was going on. If Ray was going to steal something...

"We need to catch him in the act."

I looked in my rear-view mirror at Emmett sitting in the back.

"I can hardly see him from here. Wait a minute." I turned the engine on, put on my lights—knowing Ray would probably notice through the trees—and pulled out into the road. "I'll go round to the main entrance," I told Emmett, "but park down the road so he won't see me. Then I'll sneak back in. It's dark. He won't notice."

"You clever old thing," Emmett said. "Catch the bugger at it. I never liked the look of him."

I drove around to the front of the manor, driving past the entrance as a car travelling the opposite direction turned into the driveway. It wasn't a car I recognised, and I couldn't shake the feeling that something wasn't quite right.

"A delivery?" Emmett asked as I pulled over to the side of the road to park up.

"Possibly," I said. I got out and walked the short distance back to the manor. Solar lights lined the road to the house and so I wandered off-track and onto the lawn so nobody would see me coming.

I skirted the tennis court and crouched beside some box hedging, watching as Ray lurked at the back of the building. A light came on in one of the downstairs windows and Ray moved towards the back door. A moment later, the door opened, and I raised my eyebrows when Joe Scranton appeared.

"What is he up to?" Emmett whispered.

The two men spoke briefly and then Joe beckoned Ray inside and the door closed. It had to be something to do with work, surely, but what say Joe had in Whitecott Manor's gardens I had no idea.

"Go and find out," Emmett urged me. "Persephone might be here."

I hesitated, but curiosity got the better of me and I scurried across the lawn, keeping low and hoping nobody would spot me from one of the windows. Heart pounding, I crept over to the library and peered into the window. Ray sat on the leather sofa, flat cap in hand, and I ducked out of sight when he looked towards me.

"Did he see you?" Emmett asked.

I didn't know and I didn't want to speak in case he heard me. I waited, but nothing happened, so I chanced another look. This time I caught Joe entering the room with a young woman, not Persephone, by his side. Ray jumped to his feet. Joe touched the small of the woman's back and she smiled and came forward. She took Ray's hand and they disappeared out of the library together.

Frowning, I moved away from the window and leaned back against the wall. "There's probably a simple explanation," I said quietly.

"Absolutely," Emmett agreed. "Such as?"

"Well...she could be interviewing Ray for a new job."

"Conducting the interview here? Hardly likely."

"Or she could be a long lost relative and Joe's got them back together."

"Hmm."

I looked at Emmett. "No, I don't believe it either."

I didn't know what to do. I moved to have a look in the window again when Joe came and abruptly drew the curtains, scaring the life out of me.

"You should go and ring the bell," Emmett said.

"Are you mad? What would I say?"

"I don't know; use your imagination! Say you've forgotten something. Or you want to ask for a pay rise."

I screwed up my face, letting Emmett know I thought it was a very bad idea. But... "Bollocks," I said. I had to find out what was going on.

I marched round to the front of the manor and rang the doorbell. My heart thumped against my breastbone and I cleared my throat to try to dislodge my discomfort.

I was about to ring the bell again when Joe answered. He looked at me and then past me. Clearly he'd been expecting somebody else.

"Yes?" he asked.

"Just me," I said. "Alistair. The gardener. Is Zara or David in?"

"No, sorry."

He was about to close the door, so I said quickly, "You're Joe, aren't you? The brother. I'm friends with Persephone."

Joe glanced over his shoulder into the hallway and then pulled the door closed and stepped out into the portico. "What do you want?" he asked. "Shouldn't you have gone home by now?"

"Just wanted to speak to Zara," I said. "I'll leave it." I turned to go but stopped and said, "Is Ray around?"

"Who?"

"The other gardener."

"Not seen him."

"Are you sure? I thought I saw his car still parked—"

"I've not seen him," Joe said again. "Do you mind? I'm expecting someone."

"Oh." I glanced at Emmett, who stood out in the driveway. He waved his hands at me, urging me to continue. "At your brother's house?"

"You have a problem with that?" Joe squared up to me and a frown settled on his face.

I raised my hands. "No. None of my business."

"Exactly."

I couldn't just stand there and I had the suspicion that I'd get a smack if I pried further. I turned away and walked back down the driveway, my feet crunching the gravel. Emmett fell in by my side, and together we moved over as another car headed towards the manor, a man driving and a pretty young woman in the passenger seat.

"*Something's* going on," I told Emmett.

Chapter Eleven

AT 6.30 IN the morning, my mobile phone buzzed and made me jump out of my skin. Groaning, I reached for it and then frowned when I saw it was Arthur calling me. I stifled a yawn as I answered.

"Hello?"

"You're awake, thank goodness! I need you."

I flopped back against my pillow and rubbed my face. "It's a bit early for a booty call," I said, "but if you're coming over I won't say—"

"No, it's Harriet. She's drunk as a skunk! Can't you hear her? I honestly thought I'd have to call the police. She's going to trash the place, Al, if I don't get rid of her."

I could hear a woman shouting and then the crash of something that sounded expensive. I had absolutely no idea what was going on, and it was too bloody early to make any sense of it. I rubbed my eyes. "Where are you?"

"At Granny's."

That made me sit up. "Is your grandmother okay? What's Harriet playing at? I thought she was in London."

"Granny's in hospital, Al. Two days ago. I thought I told you?"

"You didn't." I threw the duvet off and fished around in a drawer for a clean pair of boxers and socks.

"I thought I did. There's absolutely nothing to worry about. She'll be home soon. I need help with—Harry! That's fifty-year-old whisky; you can't drink that!"

"I'm on my way over," I said, pulling on my jeans one-handed. "Just...try to calm her down."

AS I PULLED up outside old Mrs Harper's cottage, I could see the light on in the lounge and hear—as soon as I got out of the car—the shouting. I hurried down the garden path and tried the door. It was unlocked, so I let myself in.

In the lounge I was confronted with the sight of Arthur and his cousin, buxom Harriet Harper, wrestling over a bottle of whisky. Harriet's usually perfect hair was a dishevelled mess of brunette rat tails, she had lipstick smeared across her face, and her eyes were red and puffy. Arthur's face was flushed pink.

"What on Earth is going on?" I demanded.

Harriet abruptly let go of the bottle, and Arthur staggered back. "Thank God you're here," he said. "She's gone absolutely mental."

Harriet folded her arms. "And who is this?"

"Alistair Ellis," I said. "The gardener. We have met." I took in the state of old Mrs Harper's lounge. Cushions were strewn across the floor, a mug had been knocked off the coffee table and was dribbling tea onto the carpet, the standard lamp lay on its side, its bulb smashed, and a vase—or what I presumed was a vase—was in pieces beside the walnut sideboard. Arthur busied himself with picking up the pieces.

"This is nothing to do with the *gardener*," Harriet said. "This is to do with my father! And my grandmother. And those *bastards* up at the manor."

"Maybe you should sit down," I said, stepping over a cushion to get to Harriet. She brushed my hand aside when I tried to help her, but she sat anyway.

"I think Harriet and her husband are getting divorced," Arthur said.

"That's none of *his* business," Harriet said. "Or yours." She pushed her hair out of her face and wiped the back of her hand across her eyes. "Who the hell calls a gardener?"

"I needed help with *you*," Arthur said. "You're intolerable."

"Look, I got out of bed especially, so..." I picked up cushions and put them back where they belonged. "Somebody tell me what's going on. Do you both think your grandmother would be happy about all this?"

Harriet huffed. "Robert and I have separated," she said. "*Not* that *you* care. I thought I'd pop over and see Granny—"

"Drunk," Arthur said.

"And talk about it with *her*."

"She's staying at the B and B," Arthur explained. "She must've been up all night drinking and then decided she'd come here and bother Granny."

"Somebody owes me money," Harriet slurred. "And seeing as though Father went and died, it'll have to be her. *She* sold our family home for a pittance."

Funny what Harriet thought a pittance. I scowled at her. "Your father died in a horrible accident. None of your sisters have complained about the money!"

"Well, that's because Isabelle," Harriet said, getting shakily to her feet, "got more. As did Princess Persephone, Daddy's little favourite."

"Isabelle was given extra for the children," Arthur said. "And Persephone's money was for her education—you'd had yours when Uncle Emmett was alive!"

Harriet blew a very unladylike raspberry at her cousin. She staggered around the coffee table, tripped over the corner of it, and fell into my arms. I held on to her as she drew in great, ugly sobs, and raised my eyebrows at Arthur.

Sorry, he mouthed to me. Then to Harriet, he said, "We need to get you back to the B and B, Harry. You need to sleep it off."

She didn't reply. I patted her head in what I hoped was a soothing way. "I'll take her," I said. "Then I'll come back and help you tidy up in here."

I left Arthur in the lounge and led a more subdued Harriet to my car. The B and B was walking distance from the cottage, being right next to the pub, but Harriet barely seemed able to stand, let alone walk, so I drove her there.

"Thank you," Emmett said, appearing in the passenger seat. "She was in a terrible state."

I looked in the rear-view mirror at Harriet snoring in the back. "She still is."

"I loved them all equally, you know," he said. "My girls."

"I know."

"As I loved you."

"Not like a son, I hope?"

Emmett laughed. "Not at all like a son! I loved you more than I ever loved my wife."

I turned the car into the small car park and turned off the engine. I didn't know how to answer Emmett, and before I could tell him how much I missed him, he had gone. Sighing, I got out of the car to help Harriet.

"Come on," I said, half carrying her to the door. "Just in time for a fry-up."

Chapter Twelve

I WAS HALF in a daze, raking leaves towards the wheelbarrow, when Zara's two little dogs came hurtling out of nowhere, barking at each other and racing round, kicking up leaves all over the place. My heart hammered. I gripped the rake tight and stared wide-eyed at the dogs, hoping they wouldn't come near me, hoping Zara was nearby to call them away.

It was stupid to be so worried about such daft little fluffballs, and I hated myself for it, but they bloody *scared* me. They were going to bite me. They were going to put me back in hospital.

They raced around the wheelbarrow. One of them tumbled the other over and then raced off, leaves sticking in its fur, the other hard on its heels. I realised I'd been holding my breath and I let it out in a shaky sigh.

Somebody chuckled and I turned to see Ray, a cigarette in his mouth and a spade in hand.

"Not scared, be 'ee?" he asked.

"No."

"Looked like you shit your pants."

I had no witty comeback, so I began raking leaves again. "Hadn't you better go and actually do something, Ray?" I asked when he stood too long watching me.

"Ah, don't worry. I'm not gonna let two little dogs frighten me off working." He chuckled and headed towards the vegetable garden where I knew he was supposed to be planting spring cabbage. As he went, I heard him mutter, "Great pansy."

"What did you say?"

He turned back to me, a big grin on his stupid face. "Think you heard me, lad. Nothing but the truth! Bloody queer."

I dropped my rake and marched over to him. "Say that again," I demanded.

Ray also dropped his spade, and he spread his arms wide, challenging me. "You're a queer. A poof. I heard they only hired you here in the first place so you wouldn't shag the wife. The Scrantons only keep you on 'cause they don't know any better. Fucking pervert."

I balled my hands into fists. "What were you snooping round here for last night?"

"What?"

"I saw you. Joe Scranton let you into the manor."

Ray jabbed a pudgy finger at me. "None of your damn business."

"Maybe I'll go and ask Zara." It was a bluff—I really didn't want to pry and I was sure it had nothing to do with Zara anyway—but when I turned away, Ray snatched at my arm.

"Cars," he said. He said it so quickly I was sure it was a lie. "We was talking about cars. Buying, selling. Would be of no interest to a gay boy like you."

"You've got no idea what interests me!"

"That blond boy interests you. Seen you and 'im in the King's Arms all cosy like."

"So?" I pulled my arm away from Ray's grip. He took the cigarette out of his mouth and flicked it into my wheelbarrow.

"Just, a soft lad like 'im might get in trouble round here, that's all."

"You leave Arthur alone," I warned.

"Ooh, Arthur, is it? Some of my ol' mates might like to teach Arthur what it's like to be a proper man. Proper soft-looking lad, he is."

I snapped. I punched Ray before I could even think about what I was doing. My fist connected with his face and blood burst from his nose. I grabbed the front of his overalls and raised my fist again.

"Alistair!"

Zara's surprised shout stopped me. I looked towards her, my fist still poised to strike Ray. Slowly, I let him go.

"He attacked me," Ray said. "You saw 'im!"

"I did," Zara agreed. Shock was written all over her face, and the look she gave me—as if I'd betrayed her in some way—made guilt strike a pang in my chest. "I think you'd better take towards the rest of the day off, Alistair. Don't you?"

I nodded. I couldn't do anything else. I couldn't even bring myself to apologise to her. I left my rake and my wheelbarrow and headed for the lane.

ALONE AT HOME I brooded in my kitchen. Bruises has popped up along my knuckles and, while part of me wished I'd punched Ray again, the other part worried about what Zara would say. I snatched up my phone, almost sent a text to Noah, but instead composed one to Arthur.

Come round mine if you're free. Need you here.

I put the phone down and waited. When I didn't get an immediate response, I got up to put the kettle on. I drummed my fingers on the work surface. Kettle was taking ages to boil. And why the hell wasn't Arthur answering me?

I was full of nervous energy. Annoyed, I grabbed my phone and stabbed out another message to Arthur.

Need you right now.

"I'm here," Emmett said, walking into my kitchen. "Talk to me."

"I don't want to talk," I said, staring at my phone. "I need to *do* something. Some*one.*"

"Charming," Emmett said. He produced a camping stool, from where I don't know, and sat on it. "You could lose your job."

"I know."

"They won't give you a warning; they'll just fire you. Ray could have you done for assault, you know."

"I know!"

My doorbell rang. I stormed past Emmett, wondering who was bothering me now, and marched down the hall. I opened the door to Arthur.

"Hello," he said, smiling at me.

"You didn't text me back," I said.

He shrugged and let himself into my home. "Your message sounded urgent, I thought it best not to waste time."

"No," I agreed. I pulled him close and kissed him, fumbling with his jacket buttons.

Arthur returned my kiss until, laughing, he pushed away my hands and removed his jacket himself. "Steady on," he said. "This wasn't cheap."

I didn't really care, but I waited for him to hang it by the door anyway and then took his hand and practically dragged him up the stairs.

In my bedroom we helped each other out of our clothes between hungry kisses. I pushed Arthur onto the bed and pressed down on top of him, watching his face as I stroked his cock, his breathing as heavy as mine.

My throat was dry with lust, and I growled as Arthur reached for my cock and pulled.

Emmett was in the room. I was aware of him standing by, silently watching. His presence angered me. So what if I was fucking his nephew? He was the one who'd gone and died on me!

I reached into the drawer beside my bed and found the lube and a condom. I flipped Arthur over and put the condom on.

"Does this turn you on?" I asked Emmett as I pushed my finger into Arthur.

"You know it does," Arthur replied, his voice muffled as he pressed his face into my pillow. He pushed back against me.

I was hornier than I'd been in a long time. I don't know if it was my anger or fear or *guilt* because Emmett watched or...

I drove into Arthur hard, pulling him up on his knees so I could fill him deeper. He moaned and reached a hand out to the headboard to steady himself, causing it to thump into the wall.

"You'll get fired," Emmett said, rounding the bed so he stood beside us. "You should be apologising to Ray, not fucking Arthur."

"Fuck. Off."

My head was full of fuzz. I gripped Arthur's hips and watched his buttocks bounce as our skin slapped together.

"You'll not find another job easily," Emmett said. "And then what will you do? It's not as if *I* can support you."

"Fuck off, Emmett!" I snapped.

"Emmett?" Arthur repeated.

I came inside him, my body twitching. I could only hold him and catch my breath as I tried to think of an explanation for what I'd just said. I licked my dry lips and swallowed.

"You didn't come," I said to Arthur, as he pushed me away.

"You mentioning my uncle rather killed my mood," he replied.

I slipped off the condom and looked at it rather than Arthur. He sat before me, naked, his face flushed pink. I leaned over the bed and tossed the condom into my wastepaper bin.

"Do you want to explain what 'fuck off, Emmett' means?"

"Uh. I don't know."

Arthur laughed, though there was no humour in it. "Were you thinking of my uncle, while we were—"

"No."

"Then you were...?"

"Look, I don't know," I said, annoyed. "I don't know why I said it. Heat of the moment thing."

"That is not usually what one says in the heat of the moment," Arthur said. He got off the bed and began gathering up his clothes. "Fuck. God. Yes. Arthur. Those are all acceptable. I fucked an American once who called me Arty. I can tolerate even that. But 'fuck off, Emmett' is really—"

"I just had this image," I said suddenly, "of your uncle watching us. I don't know why it popped into my head! I guess it's 'cause he was my boss. And you're his nephew. And we're...you know."

"Okay," Arthur said slowly. He had his trousers on now, but his shirt was still in his hands. He sat on the edge of the bed.

"I'm sorry," I said. "I was so into it...you...that he just came into my head from nowhere and I just wanted him to bugger off so I could...fuck you in peace."

Arthur raised his eyebrows at me, but there was a slight smile playing at the corner of his lips. "I see," he said. "So you were, sort of, thinking about my uncle."

I winced. "Sort of, I suppose." I offered him a hopeful smile. "Forgive me?"

"What happened today?" Arthur asked. "Why aren't you at work?"

I groaned and lay back on the bed. "That dickhead Ray was winding me up, so I punched him."

"Not a very clever thing to do."

"I know." I rubbed my face. "He was being a homophobic moron; he deserved a smack. Zara saw."

Arthur sighed. He lay next to me, propped up on his elbow so we could talk. "You need to talk to her and explain what happened," he said. "And you need to ignore Ray, no matter how much he winds you up. I'm sure you've heard all sorts of homophobic language before now."

"Yeah, well. I was defending you."

"Me?" Arthur sat up and pushed his hair out of his face. "You mean—"

"He's seen me and you together at the pub, so yeah, he knows you're gay."

Arthur cursed softly under his breath. I watched him as he fiddled with the shirt in his hands and wondered why it mattered so much.

"Your grandmother won't care that you're gay," I told him. "I don't know why you hide it. She likes me anyway. She wanted to set me up with Persephone, so she'll be happy I'm with you."

"It's not Granny I'm worried about," Arthur said. "It's my father."

"He's in Scotland!" I scoffed.

Arthur stood abruptly and put his shirt on. "That doesn't mean Granny won't speak to him," he said. "Shit! We should've been more careful. I was careful back home. Here I thought I was safe."

"Everybody knows everybody's business here. Where are you going?"

"The hospital."

"I could come?" I sat up and swung my legs over the side of the bed. "I'd like to see how the old lady's doing."

"Why would you be with me?" Arthur asked. "Granny would think it a little odd if we arrived together, don't you think?"

I shrugged.

Arthur huffed. "You stay here," he said, and he flapped his hands at me as if I were a dog and left.

"That was remarkable," Emmett said, rounding my bed to sit beside me. "You handled that like a pro, I must say. I wouldn't be surprised if you lost your boyfriend as well as your job. And all in one day!"

I grabbed a pillow and shoved it over my face as I lay back. "Fuck off, Emmett," I said.

Chapter Thirteen

I MADE SURE to get to work before Ray the next day, and I went straight to the manor to ring the bell. The dogs yapped and my heart fluttered. I'd barely had time to compose my thoughts when the door opened and David stood before me. He wore an unflattering golfing jumper and khaki trousers. I didn't know whether he *was* actually about to go golfing or not.

"Yes?" he said.

"Could I speak to Zara?" I asked. My gaze moved past David to the two little dogs standing in the hall behind him. As per usual, one gruffed at me and scurried away.

David grunted a response, closed the door a little, and turned away. I waited patiently.

David yelled, "It's the gardener for you!"

I crossed my arms and then uncrossed them again.

Zara's voice called, "Which one?" and when David returned with, "The gay one" I rolled my eyes.

Eventually, Zara opened the door. She had one of the little dogs tucked beneath her arm. "I was expecting you to speak to me yesterday," she said.

"You sent me home."

"To calm down. You could've rung me, Alistair." She put the dog down and it ran past my legs and out into the garden.

"Yeah. Sorry. I'm really, really sorry about...what you saw."

"You punched Ray in the face." Zara closed the door and stepped out into the portico. I noticed she wore leopard print slippers, and they made me smile despite the situation. "I don't think it's very funny," she said. "What on earth did you do that for? I know he's a bit of a miserable old sod, but did he deserve a smack?"

"Well...kind of."

"You're not jealous, are you, Al? 'Cause I didn't want him working here. It was David's idea."

That made me smile. "Really? No, not jealous. He's a homophobic dickhead."

"I'll have a word," Zara said. "But I need you to apologise to him, okay? I can't have my staff scrapping on the lawn!"

I nodded. "So you're not going to fire me or anything?"

Zara laughed. "Lawd, no! I wouldn't fire you, not for giving Ray a smack. You might wanna be on your best behaviour around my husband though. I'll let you off with a warning, all right? Don't do it again. And quit planting so much rhubarb. I can't stand the bloody stuff."

Emmett loved rhubarb. The words almost came out of my mouth. I scratched the back of my head and vaguely thought of ways to argue for the rhubarb, but Zara called Coco and disappeared back into the manor.

I didn't apologise to Ray. I avoided him like the plague. I hid away at the tennis court, clearing up leaves and untangling netting. It wasn't until my stomach rumbled and I thought about getting lunch that I straightened up and saw Noah.

"Hiya!" he called, flashing me a big grin. He approached the court and peered at me through the fencing. "You busy?"

"I was just heading for lunch." I dusted my hands in my overalls and joined him outside the court. "What are you doing here?"

"Doing the dogs, of course. They're drying off before I give them a clip. Thought I'd come and find you."

"Oh." I realised I was staring at him, so I looked away. "Fancy a tour?"

"Of the garden?"

"Yeah, why not?"

Noah shrugged and fell in by my side as I wandered down the path. "Probably looks better in the spring, right? Bet it's dead pretty and that."

I smiled. "It's lovely in the spring, yeah. And in the summer, all these bushes along here are filled with roses."

"I love roses, me."

I showed Noah the vegetable patch and my potting shed, the formal garden, the pond, the summer house, the arboretum, and even the compost heaps. We stopped at a bench beneath the apple tree and sat down.

"You're lucky, you know," Noah said. "Working here."

"Thought I was going to lose my job this morning. I punched Ray."

"Did ya?" Noah laughed. "Why?"

"He said something about Arthur."

"Oh right."

We were silent for a moment. Noah reached over and touched my bruised knuckles as I rested my hand on my knee, sending a little thrill through me.

"You did that to yourself?" he asked.

"Ray's got a hard head."

Noah grinned. "Can't believe *you* hit someone."

"Why not?"

"'Cause it's you! You don't look the type."

"I'll have you know I'm rough and ready," I joked.

Noah nudged me with his elbow. "I like a bit of rough and ready, me."

I laughed, but it was half-hearted and Noah, realising he probably shouldn't have said that, apologised.

"It's all right," I said, shrugging. "How's things with you and Tony?" I don't know why I brought Tony into the conversation. For my benefit, I suppose. Because I was with Arthur, and I needed Noah to remember he was with Tony.

"Fine," Noah said. He didn't sound too convinced. Before I could push for more, he said, "It's going all right with you and Arthur, then?"

"Yeah. I think. I did, kinda, mention his uncle while we were at it though."

Noah laughed loudly, making me grin. "Did ya?" he asked. "Kinky sod."

"Not like that!" I protested. "Although me and his uncle did used to..."

"No way!" Noah stared at me, his face lit up at the prospect of gossip. "You and Mr Harper? Your boss? Wasn't he, like, twice your age?"

I nodded, causing Noah to laugh in delight again. "Bloody hell," he said. "You are a dark horse, aren't ya? Does Arthur know?"

"No, and you can't tell him."

"I won't!" There was a silly grin on Noah's face. "Bloody hell. You know, I'm totally picturing you and Mr Harper at it in the potting shed now."

I looked down at my hands and hoped I wasn't blushing.

"You didn't? You dirty sod."

"He was a very good-looking guy, all right?" I said. "And he couldn't keep his hands off me."

"I bet," Noah agreed.

We grinned together. I felt comfortable with Noah in a way I didn't feel with Arthur. The realisation struck me suddenly.

"I'd better get back," Noah said, getting to his feet. "Zara will be wondering where I am. I'll catch you before I go on, yeah?"

I nodded and watched him go. As I stood to get back to work, I spotted Ray with a wheelbarrow in hand, smirking at me.

ZARA AND DAVID left before I did in the evening. I don't know where they were going, but Zara waved to me from the passenger seat of their blue car as they drove past. David either didn't see me or ignored me. I didn't fail to notice one of the little dogs pop up at the back window and bark as the car headed away. Creepy little thing.

It was too dark to work, so I downed tools and headed to my car—not bothering to say goodbye to Ray.

As I drove home, I passed Joe Scranton in his car, coming the other way. House-sitting, I thought. He had to be house-sitting.

Chapter Fourteen

THE 15TH OF November was a Sunday. I'd visit Dad and we'd have our roast dinner together. I stared at the calendar on my kitchen wall, my eyes barely focused. Three more days. Why did it have to fall on a Sunday?

"Perhaps Arthur could take your mind off it?" Emmett suggested. He sat at my kitchen table, reading a newspaper.

"I don't think Arthur wants to see me anymore."

"Noah then."

I frowned and pulled my gaze away from the calendar. "I should forget men altogether. Maybe I'll give Freddie a call and see if I can arrange a trip to London."

Emmett turned a page of his paper, more interested in *it* than me. "Freddie's a man."

"A straight man."

"My dear, why don't you spend the day with your father, have a nice lunch, and remember your mother together as any normal family would."

"Me and Dad don't work that way," I said.

I looked at the calendar again. In the box for November the 15th I'd doodled a bird. Since she'd died, I'd no longer been able to write the word's 'Mum's birthday.' And she'd always loved the birds in the garden.

I TEXT ARTHUR during my lunch break, but he didn't reply, so I returned to work with a frown on my face. In the orchard, the grease bands protecting the apple trees from the wingless winter moths had lost all their stickiness and needed replacing. I set to work, taking down the old and putting up the new—the sight of the female moths that had already fallen foul of the traps made me feel guilty, though this wasn't something I hadn't done before. Besides, it was them or my trees.

As I moved on to the next tree, something on the ground caught my eye. Off-white and rubbery. I screwed up my nose as I realised that there, in the grass, was a used condom. I straightened up and looked towards the manor, though it wasn't visible from the orchard, and wondered who the bloody hell would be having sex al fresco, in November, in Whitecott Manor's orchard.

It wouldn't be Zara and David, surely? With my gloves on, I quickly grabbed the offending article and shoved it in my black bag. Maybe some teens had snuck in. Or...Joe and Persephone? Or, god forbid, Ray? The thought of Ray doing it made me shudder. I wondered if I should let Zara know what I'd found, but then, if it *was* her and David, I didn't want to embarrass her.

I'd have to forget it. Pretend I hadn't seen it and move on.

It wasn't until later, after work, when I had an unexpected text from Noah asking how my day had been, that I decided not to forget it and brought it up again.

U what? he wrote. *Thats grim.*

I settled down in my sofa, my feet up and a mug of tea within easy reach. *Hoping it wasn't Ray's,* I sent back.

LOL! Yeh. U want me to tell zara?

No! It'll embarrass her. I paused before adding, *what are you up to?*

I reached for my tea and took a sip as I waited for Noah to text back. When my phone buzzed again, it was from a call, not a text, and I answered it with a smile on my face.

"Hiya," Noah said. "Thought I'd just ring. I'm all on me own. Tony's gone out to some work thing, and I'm stuck here like a Billy no mates."

"If it's any consolation, Arthur's still not speaking to me, so I'm on my own too."

"I could come over."

My heart beat a little faster and I sat up, carefully putting my mug on the floor. "Is that...wise?"

"What do you mean?"

I rubbed my forehead. What did I mean? I didn't trust myself enough not to make a move and, if the last kiss was anything to go by, I didn't trust Noah not to resist.

"Will Tony mind?"

"Tony's gone out! I'll be home before him. Anyway, I want your opinion on something Tony thinks is daft."

"Okay," I said, intrigued. "Yeah, come over. I'm not going anywhere."

I SHOWERED AND shaved and gave myself a spritz of cologne. Then I went down to the kitchen and put a pizza in the oven so it looked like I'd been doing something other than getting ready for Noah.

When the doorbell rang, I fiddled with my hair, shooed Emmett away, and then went to open the door.

Noah grinned at me. He wore a grey tracksuit—making me feel overdressed—and carried a large book under his arm.

"Aren't you going to let me in?" he asked after I'd probably stared at him for too long.

"Come in!" I stepped back to allow him to enter and headed down the corridor, looking back for him to follow. "I've got a pizza in the oven if you fancy any."

"All right. Thanks. You look nice. Are you going out?"

"No. I always look nice." I smiled at Noah and then peered at the book he put down on the kitchen table. It was a book on dog grooming.

"This is, like, my Bible," he said when he caught me looking. "It's got all the cuts in it. It's what I wanted to talk to you about."

I turned to the kettle. "I'm not sure how much help I'll be with that. Drink?"

"Tea. Ta." Noah sat at the table and flicked through the book. "I want to enter the National Dog Grooming Competition next year, but Tony just thinks it's daft. It'd be dead good for my business, you know?"

"I didn't know there were dog grooming competitions," I admitted. "Sounds good though, you should definitely go for it if you want to."

"Do you think I should?" He looked up at me with those honest dark eyes, and I cleared my throat and turned back to the kettle.

"Definitely. Like you say, it'd be good for business. And, you know, it sounds fun. It's good to test yourself every now and then."

"Yeah? Thanks, Al."

I placed a mug of tea in front of him, and he gave me a smile.

"What's the book for?" I asked.

"Oh! Right. Well, there's different classes, and I know a lady who'll let me borrow her toy poodle. So I thought I'd ask you which clip you liked best."

He pushed the book over to me, and I sat down and turned the pages until I found a poodle.

"That's a Standard," Noah said, leaning over to turn more pages. "This is a toy."

"Okay." I looked at the pictures of the dogs. To me, they all looked silly, but Noah was looking at me so expectantly that I just pointed to the one I thought seemed the least ugly.

Noah screwed up his nose. "That's a puppy clip. It's the easiest one there! I was thinking Dutch. Or Continental." He tapped the pictures.

"I don't like the Continental one," I said. "The poor thing's butt's all naked."

Noah laughed. "Nothing wrong with a naked arse!" he said. "Anyway, I've done that one lots. If I really want to test myself I should go for the Dutch."

"Dutch then," I said, looking at Noah rather than the pictures.

He nodded and took the book from me. "Pizza's burning," he said, and I cursed and got up to rescue it from the oven.

After we'd eaten—the pizza wasn't so bad—I washed the dishes while Noah took my calendar from the wall to work out what day the dog grooming competition would fall on next year. I was just tipping the dirty water down the sink when Noah said, "Why's there a bird on Sunday?"

I dried my hands on the tea towel. "Mum's birthday."

"Oh right." He was quiet for a moment, inspecting the doodle. Then he looked up at me and grinned. "Birdday. Like birthday."

I laughed. "She just really liked birds, that's all." I joined him at the table and sat down.

"Do you celebrate it at all?"

"Nah. I'll take her some flowers, but that's it. I'll be at my dad's anyway."

"I guess you can talk about her together, remember the good times."

I scratched my cheek and shifted in my chair. "We don't really talk about her. Too painful, I guess."

Noah stared at me for a moment before he nodded, and I knew he didn't really get why I found it so difficult. The silence became unbearable, but I couldn't think of another topic of conversation. Noah reached over and touched my hand.

Our gazes met. I knew he was only comforting me, but... Heart pounding, I leaned over and kissed him. He pulled back straight away, a look of horror on his face.

"What you doing? I'm engaged, all right?" He quickly got to his feet and tapped his ring finger, as if I'd forgotten.

"Oh, come on," I said. "You kissed me last time, remember?"

"Don't you dare," Noah said, snatching up his book. "That was a mistake. You're trying to make a move on me!"

"So what if I am!" I said, getting up. I approached Noah and he stepped back. "You can't deny there's something between us."

"Yes, I can. Look, don't touch me!" He brushed my hand aside when I reached for him. "I'm going home. You need to...think about what you've done!"

He glared at me and then stomped out, leaving me feeling faintly ridiculous.

Chapter Fifteen

AFTER WORK THE next day, I stopped by old Mrs Harper's cottage with a bag full of potatoes and a nice big celeriac. I spotted Arthur's Audi parked up the road and for a brief moment debated not going in. Then I decided that his insecurities were nothing to do with me, and he'd probably ignore me anyway. I knocked on the door and waited, kicking off my dirty boots.

Arthur answered. He hurried out onto the doorstep and pulled the door shut a little.

"I can't speak to you here," he said. "You should—"

I held up my hand. "I'm here to see your grandmother. Can I come in?"

"Oh. Well. Yes, of course."

He stepped back, and I squeezed past him in the hall, feeling smug that I'd rattled him.

"Arthur, who is it?"

"It's me, Mrs H," I called. "Alistair." I stopped in the living room doorway and raised the bag in my hand to show old Mrs Harper sitting in her armchair. "Brought some veg for you."

"Darling boy," she replied. "Arthur, take them into the kitchen, will you? And put the kettle on."

Arthur took the bag from me. His hand was cold when it brushed against mine and I wanted to warm him up. I couldn't help but watch him as he walked down the hall towards the kitchen, before I joined his grandmother in the living room.

I sat on the sofa. A fire cracked and popped in the fireplace and the room was comfortably warm. Vaguely, I wondered why Arthur's hands were so cold and if he was coming down with something.

"Harriet tells me you helped take care of her while she was being a drunken pain in the arse," old Mrs Harper said.

"I gave her a lift, that was all," I said. I noticed the old lady's right hand trembled as she rested it on the arm of the chair, and I frowned.

Seeing my concern, she clasped her hands in her lap and tutted at me. "I'm quite all right," she said. "I'm an old woman, Alistair, everything is perfectly normal."

"I know, I—"

There was a crash from the kitchen, and I jumped up from my seat to see what Arthur was doing. When I entered the kitchen, he was leaning against the kitchen worktop, pale and shaky, with the tea tray dropped on the floor by his feet.

"Hey," I said, joining him. I touched his forehead to check for a fever. "What happened? You okay?"

"Dizzy spell, that's all," Arthur replied, brushing my hand away. "I've made such a bloody mess."

He bent to pick up the tray, but I stopped him. "I'll do that. Go sit down."

"No, no—"

"Arthur." I took his hands when he moved towards the tray again and held on to him. "Are you all right? You're freezing cold."

"Don't fuss." He gave my hands a brief reassuring squeeze before he pulled away. "I moved too quickly, my head spun, and I dropped the tray. Help me clean up."

I knelt to collect broken bits of crockery, watching Arthur in concern as he joined me. He glanced at me and then away. "I spoke to your friend, Ray," he said quietly.

"He's not my friend."

"He told me you've been flirting with the dog groomer. Noah."

I hated Ray. Bloody gossip. I stood to get some kitchen towel to mop up the spilt tea.

"I'm flirty," I said, shrugging. "Does it matter? We're not a couple anyway, are we?"

"Shh!" he hissed at me. "Granny will hear." He picked up the tray and put it in the sink. "No, I don't suppose we are. You won't mind, then, that Tony and I kissed."

"What?" I grabbed his arm when he turned away from me. "When?"

"At the karaoke. When we went to the bathroom. I pushed him away, but perhaps I should've just let him fuck me in one of the cubicles."

"He's engaged!" I was incensed, furious with Tony for doing that to Noah—furious he would try to take Arthur from me. I became aware I was gripping Arthur tight, and when I let him go, he rubbed his arm.

We both turned together when old Mrs Harper cleared her throat. "What on Earth is going on in here?" she asked.

Arthur was all apologetic smiles. "Sorry, Granny. I'm terribly clumsy. Alistair was helping me clean up."

"Well do it quietly," she said. "If you're going to have a lover's tiff, at least wait until you're somewhere private."

Arthur flushed pink. I scratched my cheek, embarrassed. "We're not," Arthur started, laughing a little, "I mean...that is...I'm not *gay*. We're not lovers. And we're not having a tiff. I—"

"Arthur, do give me some credit. I've been around much longer than you have. I will not allow you to have a spat in my home."

"Sorry, Mrs H," I said. "I think maybe I should just go."

"Of course, Alistair. Thank you."

I deposited the wet kitchen towel in the bin, and after offering Arthur a quick apologetic smile, I made my way out, though as I closed the door I heard Arthur say, "*You can't tell Father.*"

LATER, I LAY in bed with my phone in hand, vaguely watching Emmett set up a chessboard on the barely used desk in the corner of my room.

"Do you think he's ill?" Emmett asked.

"I don't know. I hope not."

"Text him."

I sent a text to Arthur: *You ok?* And waited.

"You ought to warn Ray to keep his nose out of your business," Emmett said. "Black or white?"

"I'm not playing," I said. "I'm going to ignore Ray."

My phone beeped.

Yes. Granny knows about us but she won't tell my father.

I looked up as Emmett moved a chess piece and studied the board.

"Do you think Arthur should just come out?" I asked him.

"I think Arthur should be able to do whatever he wishes. Straight people don't run around telling people they're straight."

"Yeah but...they don't hide it, do they." My thumb hovered over my phone. I scratched my chin thoughtfully, feeling the day's stubble under my nails, before typing, *Was worried about you earlier.*

Nothing to worry about x

The kiss put my mind at ease, and I abandoned my phone by my side. "Come on then," I said, joining Emmett. "Kick my arse at chess."

Chapter Sixteen

ON SATURDAY I bumped into Persephone in the florist's in the village. I hadn't spotted her in there. I was waiting for the lady who owned the shop to stop gossiping on the phone and help me pick out some flowers for Mum when somebody grabbed my arm.

"Al! It *is* you! I haven't seen you since..."

"Your grandmother's," I said, smiling. "You were telling us all about Joe."

"That's it. How are you?"

Persephone looked beautiful. Her cheeks had filled out a little and she was flushed a pretty pink. Being in a relationship obviously agreed with her, whatever misgivings old Mrs Harper and myself might have had about Joe Scranton.

"Good," I said. "Busy."

"Do you still sing?"

The florist was off the phone now, and she served Persephone who, I noticed, was buying pink and blue ribbons.

I nodded. "I still sing."

"How lovely!" She deposited her ribbons in her handbag before taking my arm to lead me away from the florist, though I really wanted to get Mum's flowers.

"I have a secret," she said. "Can I tell you?"

"Okay," I said slowly, not sure I wanted to hear it. "Go on."

"I'm pregnant."

I gawped at her. Behind her, Emmett popped up, his eyebrows disappearing into his hairline. "She's what?"

"Pregnant," I said. "Wow. Uh..."

"I've not told Joe yet," Persephone said. "You mustn't tell him. I want to make sure the moment's right, make sure it's romantic."

I nodded dumbly. I wish she hadn't told me; it wasn't any of my business, and I could only stare at Emmett, wishing he were real.

"My little girl is pregnant," he said. "Princess Persephone. You have to take care of her, Al. You must make sure she's okay."

"I'm sure Joe will do that," I told him.

"Will do what?" Persephone asked.

I forced my gaze back to her and smiled. "Make sure it's romantic. The moment. You know. Just by being there."

She nodded, though she knew as well as I did that I wasn't making any sense. She patted my arm. "I must dash. Give my love to Granny if you see her before I do."

"I will." Great. Old Mrs Harper would *not* take that news well. Persephone throwing away her education and procreating with Joe Scranton? Hopefully it wouldn't cause a heart attack. I sighed and returned to the florist to buy Mum's flowers.

SUNDAY. I WOULD spend the afternoon at my dad's, eating a roast dinner in silence. We would both be missing Mum keenly, but neither of us would talk about her. The flowers I'd bought for her would stay in my car—I wouldn't risk taking them in with me and reminding Dad she ever existed—until I was ready to head home, and then I would stop by the cemetery to stand in silence beside her grave.

For now though, it was morning, and I lay on my bed and flicked through the names in my phone. I desperately wanted to contact Noah, if only to tell him how sorry I was for making a move on him, but I didn't want to remind him I'd done that, so I texted Arthur instead.

How are you feeling? x

"Do you think he knows Persephone's pregnant?" Emmett asked. He stood beside my wardrobe, holding one of my shirts up to his chest.

"Arthur? I don't know. She seems to be telling everybody, apart from Joe. That shirt's too young for you, by the way."

"I'm not sure pink is quite my colour anyway."

"It's salmon," I said. My phone buzzed, and I looked at it. Arthur had texted me back.

Exhausted. I'm going to the doctors tomorrow. x

"Arthur's not well," I told Emmett, frowning in concern. "Do you think I should go over and see him? I'll ask him."

I typed, *Do you want me to come over? Do you need anything? x*

"Don't fuss the poor boy," Emmett said. "He doesn't need mothering."

"I'm not mothering him!" I wondered if he was up for some loving—if he was already in bed it wasn't like he'd have to get up, and sex was good for making people feel better anyway. I needed somebody to take my mind off the upcoming afternoon.

My phone lit up with a new message and I read it twice before I realised it was from Noah, not Arthur.

Say happy b'day to ur mum from me x

I smiled a little, touched that he'd remembered.

Thanks. I'm going to take her some flowers this afternoon. I'll say hi from you.

Want me to come with? x

I frowned at the phone. "Why would he do that?" I said to Emmett. "He's messing with my mind. He doesn't want me, and yet he'll come and visit Mum's grave with me. That's not normal, right?"

Emmett sat on the edge of my bed. "My dear, you should tell him about Tony. I'm sure he'd soon jump in your bed if he knew his fiancé was a cheating arsehole."

Maybe. Was that a decent thing to do though? Break Noah's heart so I could get some revenge sex? I scratched the side of my face.

My phone buzzed again. Arthur this time.

I'm okay, thanks. Might need cheering up tomorrow after I've seen the doctor though, got a blood test. :) xx

Distracted, I texted back.

You'll be fine x

God, since when did my love life become this complicated? I felt like I had two men on the go, though in reality I had neither.

"If I were young again," Emmett said, "and alive, I would fuck both of them."

I snorted at that. "No, you wouldn't. You had to be drunk to come on to me. And Arthur is your nephew!"

He rolled his eyes at me. "Of course not Arthur. I'm simply saying if I had two young men interested in me, I would try them both out."

"Since when did you become so uninhibited?"

"Death makes you bold."

I turned back to my phone. Noah wanted to see me. He wouldn't ask to come with me, on such a personal errand, if he didn't want to spend time with me.

OK, I texted. *Meet at mine at 3 x*

THE SUNDAY ROAST came and went with no incidents. I mentioned Mum, briefly, letting Dad know I would take some flowers to her that afternoon, and he'd given me a nod and a gruff "Good lad" and that was it. I went home and waited for Noah, and I debated changing my clothes but didn't feel much like dressing up. I didn't feel much like doing anything.

Grief had numbed me. Emmett hadn't appeared again and I wanted the day to be over already so I could curl up in bed and wake up to a normal day. My head was weirdly heavy, as if it carried around too much pain. The feeling frustrated me, and I glowered at the ceiling.

When Noah knocked on the front door, it made me jump out of my bloody skin. Sighing and wishing I'd decided to visit Mum on my own, I wandered down the stairs and opened the door. Noah grinned at me. I noticed he'd shaved a pattern into the hair on the sides of his head, making him look like a proper townie, and I smiled a little.

"Hiya," he said. "Cheer up! Oh yeah...sorry. Ignore me. You ready?"

"One sec." I nipped into the kitchen to collect the flowers I'd left in the sink and then headed back to Noah. "We can walk from here," I told him as I closed the door.

"You didn't mind me coming, did you?" Noah asked as we walked down the pavement together.

"No. I would've said."

"Oh right."

We walked in silence for a bit, past a row of cottages—a couple with thatched roofs—and then cut through the park, passing the sorry-looking kids' play area where one young mother dutifully pushed her toddler on the swing.

"How was dinner?" Noah asked.

"All right," I said. "Same as usual." I just wanted to walk in silence. I didn't mind that he was with me—in fact, I wanted to take his hand—but I didn't want small talk.

"Tony's gone out," he said. "Sometimes it'd be nice to do something together at the weekend, you know? But he's just gone out in a huff. Had a bit of an argument this morning. He never wants to do anything!"

I frowned. "Is that the reason you offered to come with me? Because you had a row with Tony?"

"No!" Noah grabbed my arm and I stopped walking. "Is that what you think?"

I shrugged.

"No, all right? I knew it was your mum's birthday and thought you might like a bit of company."

It didn't really matter, I supposed. Maybe Noah was spending time with me to make Tony jealous. Maybe he genuinely cared. I found thinking about it too difficult for my fuddled brain. Instead, I pointed to the gates to the graveyard across the road.

"I don't think I've ever really been to a cemetery," Noah said as we crossed over. "Don't really know many dead people. And most people get cremated nowadays, don't they? You just scatter them in the wind and they float off somewhere."

I opened the squeaky gate and waved Noah in ahead of me. Then I headed off down the path that led to Mum's grave, gripping the flowers tight.

"Spooky, isn't it?" Noah said. "Well, not so much in the daylight, but I reckon it'd be dead spooky at night. Hey, we should come back here later and look for ghosts or something. You fancy it?"

"No," I said, frowning.

"Oh. Is your boss buried here too, or did he get cremated?"

I rubbed my forehead. "No, he's buried at St. Mary's. Different church."

"Oh right."

We stopped beside my mum's grave, and I stared at the tombstone. *Samantha Ellis, beloved wife and mother.*

Noah had shut up, so I laid the flowers on the grave and wished her a happy birthday. When I straightened up, Noah took my hand and gave it a little squeeze.

"I bet she's watching," he said, his voice soft. "You know. Wherever she is. Heaven. I bet she's watching you."

"Yeah," I said. Noah's hand was warm in mine; I wanted to hold it forever, but he let go and thrust both his hands into his ugly bomber jacket pockets.

It annoyed me suddenly. It felt like he was playing with me, toying with my emotions, touching me and kissing me and coming with me to my mother's grave when *he* was engaged.

"There's something you should know," I said. "About Tony. He came on to Arthur. Kissed him."

My heart pounded. Noah took a step back from the grave side.

"You what?"

I looked at him, at the frown lining his beautiful face.

"When we were at the karaoke. Tony kissed Arthur. Arthur told me."

"Oh yeah? You sure it wasn't your little posh boy who came on to him?"

"No!" I said. "Arthur's not like that." Arthur *was* like that, I realised, but for the purpose of the argument, Arthur was a saint.

"Yeah, well neither's Tony!"

"Tony looks like a player," I scoffed.

"How dare you, right?" Noah said, jabbing a finger at my chest. "You don't know him! And, in case you've forgotten, you came on to me last time we met, so you're no angel."

"And in case *you've* forgotten, you kissed me before that!"

"Yeah? Well that was a mistake."

"Good! It was a mistake kissing you, too. I'd much rather be with Arthur!"

"And I'd rather be with Tony."

"Good!" We glared at each other. Blood pumped through me, pulsing loud in my ears. I'd balled my hands into fists. God, I really wanted to—

Noah kissed me. He lunged at me, grabbed my face between his hands, and kissed me. It took only a moment before I was kissing him back, my mouth opening hungrily to his, his tongue wet and warm. I grasped hold of his hips and pressed him close.

"No, stop. Stop." Noah pulled back. He wiped a shaky hand across his lips. "I can't do this."

"You can," I said. "You are!"

"No, I'm *with* Tony. And you're with Arthur."

"I'm not, not really."

"But I am with Tony. We're engaged." He twisted his ring, as if to remind himself. I wanted him to take the stupid thing off and throw it away.

"There's something between us," I said. "You can't deny it. You feel it too. There's *something*—"

"No," Noah said. "Look, I'm sorry. I can't do this." He raised his hand to stop me stepping towards him, and then he turned and walked away.

I stared after him, realising I'd have to hang around, otherwise I'd just end up trailing him back to my house.

Chapter Seventeen

AT WORK RAY busied himself repairing one of the glass panes in the greenhouse, so I made sure I was as far from him as possible and lingered near the front of the manor, planting hundreds of daffodil bulbs along the driveway so it'd look lovely come spring.

On my lunch break, Arthur sent me a text to let me know he'd get the results of his blood test soon, and I replied asking that he let me know how he got on. I didn't hear from Noah, and I tried not to think about him at all. I was just walking across the lawn to take my lunchbox back to my car when somebody shouted my name.

Turning, I spotted Tony marching towards me. He wore a smart grey suit paired with a red skinny tie, which looked at odds with the angry frown on his face.

"Can I help you?" I asked.

"You've been telling tales to Noah," he said, stopping just short of me. "You keep your nose out of *my* business, and stay away from him!"

I laughed. "I should be saying the same to you. Stay away from Arthur."

He grabbed the front of my overalls and tugged me close. His eyes were wide. "You kiss my man again, and I'll kill you."

"He told you that?" I hadn't meant to sound so surprised. Noah had told Tony what had happened—so I wasn't a secret; I was a mistake. My heart sank.

"Of course he did. You don't touch him again, you hear me?"

I ripped Tony's hands away and pushed him. "You kissed Arthur! How dare you—"

Pain shot through my jawbone as Tony's fist connected with my cheek. Straightening up, I hit him back, throwing my weight behind my punch. We grappled, grabbing each other's clothes like a couple of drunken women outside a nightclub, and ended up on the ground. I fought Tony's hands as he straddled me and managed to get a jab in on his ribs.

"Noah is mine, do you hear me?" he yelled. "Nobody else touches him. You and your filthy hands—"

I jabbed him again in the ribs and shoved him off. His suit was covered in mud now, the jacket torn at the sleeve. I hated him. It was my turn to pin him down, and as I pulled back my fist to smack him in the mouth, a jet of very cold water hit me in the chest and face.

I hurried to my feet and held out my hands protectively—though it didn't help—as Ray turned the hose on the both of us. When Tony was up, dripping wet, his shoulders heaving with rage, Ray switched off the hose.

"Bloody queers," Ray said. "Bugger off the pair of you. Go on! Get out of here."

I said nothing. I snatched up my lunchbox and squelched back to my car.

"What did that achieve?" Emmett asked, strolling by my side as if we were out on a nice walk in the park.

"I didn't start that," I said, pulling my car door open and slinging the lunchbox into the back. "Tony is insane. Did you hear him? Talking about Noah as if he's a possession." I shrugged off my soaking overalls, peeled them down my legs, and threw them into the car.

"You're the one talking to a dead man," Emmett commented.

I glared at him before getting into the car and slamming the door.

IT WASN'T UNTIL the evening that I realised I'd left my phone at work. It had to be sitting on the bench still where I'd eaten my lunch. Unless Ray had taken it. Or Tony. Hopefully Zara would've picked it up and taken it in for me, but I couldn't settle, so I hopped in the car and drove back to the manor.

As I wasn't intending to stay long, I turned into the driveway to park out the front, but as soon as I got past the gates, I saw cars had already filled most of the space in front of the building and figured Zara and David had to be entertaining.

Zara must've skipped class with the dogs, I mused, as I squeezed my car into a space next to a Nissan Qashqai and a bright yellow VW Polo. I didn't blame her—I'd much rather spend an evening boozing it up with my mates than being surrounded by yapping dogs too.

After I grabbed my torch from the back of my car, I headed off into the grounds to check my phone wasn't still where I'd left it. I didn't want to disturb the Scrantons when they were busy if I didn't have to.

Cold air blew into my face and made me tense my jaw. A niggling voice in the back of my mind told me Tony had taken my phone and was now reading all the messages I'd exchanged with Noah. No—it'd be where I'd left it. Why would Tony...

Giggling behind the hedge. God, I hoped it wasn't Zara and David having al fresco sex again. It was too damn cold, wasn't it? Horny buggers.

I hesitated for only a moment before clearing my throat and rounding the hedge. My torchlight blinded the woman sitting on the bench, and I lowered it as she shielded her eyes. The guy with her jumped to his feet. I didn't recognise them.

"Sorry," I said. "You haven't seen a phone out here, have you?"

"Nah, mate," the man said. He was tall and far too skinny. He stood awkwardly and scratched the side of his spotty face as if he were embarrassed.

The woman—wearing a low-cut top (she must've been freezing) and tight leather trousers—grinned up at me. "You maybe lost it in one of the rooms, lovely?"

"No, I've not been in. I'm not a guest. I work here."

She laughed, though I didn't know what was funny. The man reached for her hand and tugged her to her feet. "We should go back inside," he said.

"He's handsome. He could join us," the woman said. She'd not made any attempt to lower her voice, and her companion glared at her.

"No, I'm not...into that," he muttered.

"Could you tell Zara I'm here?" I asked. "I'm Alistair. I left my phone out here earlier. I think she might've picked it up."

"Who's Zara?" the woman asked. She turned to the man. "Zara. Is she the one with the big tits?"

"Joe's sister-in-law," the man said. Then to me, "Zara's not in. Sorry." He turned away, pulling the woman with him.

"David then?" I called after them.

The woman giggled again, and the man grunted a reply and waved a hand vaguely back at me that I took to mean yes, he'd let David know.

Sighing, I turned back to the bench and shone my light beneath it. The reflection off my phone caught my eye, and I reached under to grab it. Relieved, I shoved it in my pocket and made my way back to my car. I doubted David would come out to see me, even if the strange man and his girlfriend let him know I was there.

I wondered why Zara had chosen dog class over a party with her mates.

Chapter Eighteen

IT WAS A Thursday afternoon—I'd just nipped into the village to pick up some twine from the shop when I spotted Arthur drive by in his Audi. I wandered up the road towards old Mrs Harper's cottage, watching Arthur pull up. He stepped out of the car and spotted me, raising a hand briefly in greeting.

I smiled and walked over to him. "Hey. You okay?"

"Absolutely," Arthur replied. I noticed he looked a little less pale, though his cheeks were already beginning to turn pink with the cold. "You're staring," he said.

"Oh. Sorry. You look better. Have you had your results?""

He smiled at me and jangled the car keys in his hand.

"Anaemic," he said. "Nothing to worry about. I should eat more meat."

I wanted to make a filthy comment but wasn't sure how well it'd go down. Arthur chuckled—realising exactly what I was thinking—and I laughed too.

"I'm glad you're feeling better," I said. "I should head back to work. Say hi to Mrs H."

"I will do. Al?" He took my arm as I turned away. "I can come over later. If you'd like."

"I would like that," I said, gazing at him. "Yeah."

MY KITCHEN SMELLED of Bolognese and I poured a little more red wine into the sauce before I shimmied over to the radio to turn the volume up. I sang along with Beyoncé.

"You're in a good mood," Emmett commented.

I turned briefly to him, sitting at my table with a napkin tucked into his shirt. "I am," I agreed. "I'm going to get laid."

"Charming. Arthur's still my nephew."

"Still don't care." I stirred the Bolognese and checked on the pasta. "The thing I like about Arthur is he's free and single and horny. That's three things. He's handsome—runs in the family, of course—and he hasn't got a stupid fiancé hanging about, flipping out if I dare touch him."

"You're using him," Emmett said. "You're using him for sex because you can't have Noah."

"Arthur *wants* sex," I said. "You're not staying for dinner, by the way." I dipped a spoon into the sauce and tasted it, burning my tongue. Emmett scowled at me; I could feel his eyes boring a hole in the back of my head, but I ignored him and headed off to answer the door when the bell rang.

I opened the door to Arthur. He'd made an effort, I noticed. He wore smart grey trousers and a thick woollen coat, paired with a red scarf that went really well with his blond hair. As I leaned forward to peck him on the cheek, I caught whiff of his aftershave—cedar wood and grapefruit.

"You're cooking?" Arthur asked, taking off his scarf.

"Spaghetti Bolognese," I said, hanging his coat by the door. "Is that okay?"

"Lovely."

I turned the music down once we reached the kitchen and gave the food a quick stir before dishing it up. Emmett had buggered off, I was pleased to notice, and I smiled at Arthur as he took a seat where his uncle had previously occupied.

"Bolognese has meat in it so it's high in iron, right?" I asked, taking the plates to the table.

"It's terribly sweet that you're thinking of me like this," Arthur said.

I shrugged and poured him a glass of wine before taking my seat opposite. "Trying to get back in your good books," I joked.

We ate quietly, exchanging only a few words, and had I not been so distracted with the idea of having sex at the end of the meal, I'm sure I would've found the whole thing awkward. I took the plates to the sink once we'd finished eating, and Arthur joined me, circling his arms around my waist.

"You're not going to wash the dishes now, are you?" he asked. He popped the button on my trousers.

"I thought I might, yeah," I replied innocently. "I don't think they can wait."

I tensed as Arthur slipped a cold hand into my pants. "I'm sure they can."

"Uh huh." I leaned back against him, tilting my head so he could kiss my neck. He turned me around, took down my trousers and boxers, and knelt before me. I touched his soft blond hair and then closed my eyes as he ran his tongue up my shaft.

My mouth hung open a little, and I reached back to grip the edge of the worktop to steady myself. Arthur's hot mouth was a wonderful, stark contrast to his cold hands.

Swallowing hard, I opened my eyes to look down at him. But another person caught my eye—Emmett, sitting up at the table and reading a newspaper as if nothing was happening.

"Couldn't you take it to the bedroom?" Emmett asked, not lifting his attention from the paper.

I wondered if that'd make any difference, or if he would just decide to haunt me every time Arthur and I got it on.

"No," I growled.

Arthur took my dick out of his mouth and pumped me with his fist instead. He had a wicked glint in his eye. "Oh come on," he said, "I've hardly started. You can last a little longer."

Emmett folded his paper and turned on the chair. "Yes, come on, Alistair. I know you can last much longer than that."

"Let's go upstairs," I said, pulling Arthur up and ignoring Emmett.

Arthur put his arms around me and pressed close. "Can't you just bend me over the kitchen table?"

Behind him, Emmett raised his eyebrows. I frowned. "The bed is so much comfier."

"I really don't think I can make it upstairs," Arthur said, pouting. He rubbed against me. and I groaned.

"But...upstairs..." I shut up as Arthur slid down my body and took me into his mouth once more.

I stared at Emmett, willing him to go away. He smiled back at me. *I'm screwing his nephew.*

"Oh god. Emmett's watching!" I blurted out, pushing Arthur away. I hurriedly shoved my dick back into my pants. "We really need to go upstairs. I can't—"

"Uncle Emmett is dead," Arthur said slowly. He wiped a hand across his mouth and stood up. His hair stuck up on one side where I'd been holding him. "And I'm sure he's far too busy in Heaven to be watching *us*. Why are you thinking about my uncle again?"

"He'll think you're crazy," Emmett said. "Or perverted."

"I'm not...I just..." I didn't know what to say. Suddenly, I wasn't quite so horny.

Arthur sighed. "I'm going to head off," he said, flattening his hair. "Give me a call when you're able to fuck without bringing my uncle into the equation."

All I could do was nod stupidly as Arthur turned and left the room. The front door closed with a soft click. I wondered if I should see a shrink after all.

At the table, Emmett lifted a teacup to his lips.

Chapter Nineteen

IT WAS FRIDAY the fourth of December. I stood in the queue in the corner shop, staring at a poster on the message board which announced the Christmas lights switch on at the weekend. The council had already erected a ratty-looking tree on the village green and a string of dirty bulbs hung around it. I wondered what old Mrs Harper thought of it, as she'd have a good view from her lounge window. She'd probably not be impressed. I scratched the stubble on my cheek and moved forward as the lady before me paid for her shopping and left. The woman behind the counter smiled as I plonked my goods—a pint of milk, a packet of bacon, and a bottle of brown sauce—in front of her.

"I was thinking," she said; she had a lovely Welsh lilt, "of getting in some of those gay magazines for you, Al."

She'd worked at the shop for years. I think she knew my dad, but I could never remember her name. I gave her a puzzled smile. "Why?"

"Wouldn't you like something to read?"

"I read the paper," I said.

"Oh yes, of course you do, love, but there's not very many gays in the paper, is there? I'll get you in one of those magazines."

I opened my wallet and fished out a crumpled fiver.

"It's all right. Thank you." I waved the note at her, and she took it cheerfully and stashed it in the till.

"I just don't want you getting lonely."

"What?"

"Well, it's almost Christmas now and I started thinking about all the people in the village on their own and I couldn't help but worry. Your old dad's on his own too."

"Dad's fine," I said, taking my change. I frowned, wondering where all this had come from. In my pocket, my phone buzzed.

"Is he?" she asked. "I mean, do you think he'd mind if—"

"Sorry," I said, fishing my phone from my pocket. *Noah calling.* "I've got to get this." I turned and headed out of the shop. Noah hadn't contacted me in ages and I'd not seen him at the manor for a while.

Outside, rain drizzled down and I hooked up my hood and answered the phone. "Hello?"

"Al? It's Noah. Are you home? Please be home. I need to see you. Are you home? It's Tony. And me. It's me and Tony. Are you home?"

"Slow down," I said. "I'm almost home. Give me ten minutes. Are you okay?"

"No." I could hear a tremble in his voice. "We've split up."

WHEN I REACHED my house, I spotted Noah's van parked outside. I paused before knocking on his window, my heart fluttering at the thought a dog might be inside and bark at me, but I knocked and Noah rolled down the window.

"Come inside," I told him. His eyes were bloodshot and his nose shiny. "I'll put the kettle on."

We entered my house in silence. I hung up my jacket and closed the front door as Noah wandered down the hall to the kitchen. As I joined him, he rubbed his finger, and I noticed he'd removed his engagement ring. Frowning, I put the kettle on.

"It's just...I can't take it anymore, you know?" Noah picked at the corner of the table with his nail and then folded his hands in his lap. "He's always working, and he's got an important job, I get that, but mine's important too, right?"

I nodded. "Yeah. I mean, think of all the dogs who'd be...uh...matted and—"

"It's important to me. And I love Tony, I do. But whenever we do finally go out together, he gets so *jealous*! I can't be controlled like that."

Our gazes met when he glanced at me. I turned away when the kettle boiled and plopped two teabags into a couple of mugs.

"I 'eard what he did to you," Noah said. "I'm sorry."

I shrugged. I didn't really know why Noah had come to me. What was he expecting?

"Anyway, it's over," he continued. "We're done. I can't marry him."

"I'm sure you'll sort things out." I placed a mug in front of him and sat opposite him at the table. "You still love each other, don't you?"

"I guess."

I smiled at how petulant his statement was. Noah obviously loved Tony—what Tony felt I didn't know. I wondered if he'd ever loved him, or if it was always a case of Noah being his possession.

Noah sniffed and sipped his tea.

"Had to see you," he said eventually. "Didn't know who else to talk to. Well, Mum's been great and Dani told me to go out and shag as many guys as I could, but, I dunno. Just wanted to talk to you."

"Just talk?" I said carefully.

Noah rolled his eyes. "I'm not gonna jump into bed with you, all right? What sort of man do you take me for? I'm not easy."

I held up my hands. "Okay! I didn't mean—"

"I know. Sorry."

I drank my tea, picked dirt from beneath my fingernails, and stared out the kitchen window at the rain. "Do you think you will sort things out?" I asked.

"Maybe. I don't know."

I nodded and gazed at Noah. He appeared more relaxed now, hugging his tea between his hands, his lips twitched into a smile when he looked at me.

"S'nice this," he said. "Sitting having a cuppa with you."

It was nice. Comfortable. I had to look away when my cheeks grew hot, and I cleared my throat and lifted my mug to my lips again.

"Do you want to come and see one of my sister's shows at the weekend with me?" Noah asked.

"I was going to ask if you wanted to watch the Christmas lights switch on with me," I said. "But yours is better."

"We can do both?"

"Yeah?" I nodded. "I'd like that."

"Maybe you can do some singing," Noah said. "At the switch on. You could sing Silent Night or something."

I laughed. "I think I'd look a bit odd if I just started singing on my own."

"Don't they do, like, carols or something?"

"They might do."

Noah grinned at me, and I felt like bursting into song there and then.

Chapter Twenty

DESPITE THE FACT that Saturday evening was as cold as it had been in a long time, Noah turned up on my doorstep wearing a tracksuit and hoody. He didn't look bothered by the weather, though, and dragged me out the house as soon as I'd grabbed my duffle coat.

"It's really not going to be that exciting," I warned him. "The lights aren't even that nice."

"Don't care," Noah said. "It's nice just to be out doing stuff."

My breath puffed in front of me as I walked, making it look as if I was smoking. I had my hands thrust deep into my pockets, but I really wanted to take hold of Noah's.

"Aren't you cold?" I asked.

"Nah. I'll warm up when we get there anyway with all the bodies around."

I chuckled. "How busy do you think it's going to be?"

When we reached the village green, there were actually more people there than I'd been expecting. I noticed a little merry-go-round had been set up for the kids, and a hot dog cart had parked up on the other side of the road. A group of carol singers converged near the tree, and beside them stood a man holding a reindeer by the halter.

Noah tugged my arm to point the animal out to me. "Dead good this, innit?" he said. "Dead villagey."

"Yeah, dead villagey," I agreed, amused by his excitement. I wondered if they did this sort of thing up in Manchester. Probably not as quaint. I was just about to offer to go and buy us hotdogs when I spotted my dad through the crowd. I would've waved if I'd caught his eye, but noticed he seemed preoccupied with someone.

"Isn't that your dad?" Noah asked, realising what I was looking at. "Who's the lady?"

I frowned. "The lady from the shop," I said. She was laughing, her face alive with amusement—even my dad was smiling; he was *smiling*.

"They look friendly," Noah commented.

"They do." I half wanted to go over to see how my dad'd react with me there, but somebody else caught my eye—a man pushing his way past the people carrying a ridiculous tuba. I laughed when I realised it was Emmett.

"What's funny?" Noah asked.

"Uh..." I watched as Emmett joined the carollers and lifted the tuba to his lips. "Nothing. Just happy."

"Yeah?" Noah said. "Me too."

I smiled at him, and he held my gaze. A man's voice carried above everybody else's, but I missed what he said. When the crowd cheered, I realised we'd just missed the lights going on. Noah and I turned to the tree and clapped, though I personally didn't think it was worth cheering. The singers began *Away in a Manger.*

"You know the lights, right," Noah said, thoughtfully, "why don't they set the tree on fire?"

"They don't get hot enough," I said.

"Oh right. You think the tree'd go right up. Aren't pines like, ninety percent resin or something?"

I just gave him a bemused smile and headed towards the hot dog stall.

"Come on," I said, "I'll get you something to warm you up."

NOAH INVITED ME back to his home so I could meet his sister ahead of her show on Sunday, so I got in my car and followed his van to Yeovil.

His house sat on the outskirts of the town, next to a twenty-four-hour garage. It looked nice enough, if a little tatty—a red-bricked end-terrace with a small garden hidden behind a wall and steps leading up to the front door. We parked on the road and Noah waited for me as I got out of my car.

I gave him a nervous grin.

"They won't mind me just turning up? It's quite late."

It was 9:30. An outside light came on as Noah walked up the steps. "Nah," he said. "They'll all be sitting round the telly."

I nodded. Noah put his key in the lock and suddenly a dog barked—what sounded like a very large dog—and I jumped out of my skin. I stood, frozen on the bottom step.

"Noah…"

He turned to look at me. "S'all right. He won't hurt you," he said. "It's Hercules; he's soft as shit."

"I have allergies, remember?"

"It's just a sniffle, right? Come on." Noah unlocked the door and a very large, terrifying-looking grey dog pushed into him. He grabbed the animal's collar and dragged it back. I couldn't move, this thing—I later discovered the breed was a cane corso—was the size of a horse.

"Noah…"

"Come on!"

I couldn't. I couldn't move. My heart pounded so much it was almost painful—this beast would know I was afraid and it'd bite me, I knew it.

"Al!"

The dog barked and I jumped. A woman's voice called, "Will you shut the door? You're letting all the cold air in!"

"You're frightened," Noah said. "He won't hurt you, I promise."

"I'm not…" I realised it was pretty obvious I was terrified. I couldn't deny it any more. "I have a phobia, dogs…"

"Really?" Noah sounded as if I'd said the most ridiculous thing ever. I could only nod. "He won't hurt you," he said again.

I took an involuntary step backwards towards my car. "I can't come in. I can't. It's a phobia. It's irrational—"

"Mum! Call Herc!" Noah yelled.

His mother called the dog and it disappeared out of sight. Noah pulled the door closed but I was too strung out to do anything but stare at where the animal had stood. I'd shown myself up. He'd never fall for me now—the dog groomer and the cynophobic gardener.

"Mum can shut him in the kitchen for a bit," Noah said. "You'll be all right."

They'd laugh at me. The soft country gay boy afraid of dogs.

"Come on." Noah wandered down the steps and took hold of my hand. "I'll look after you."

He grinned at me, and though I knew he was taking the piss, I really believed he would.

"Sorry," I muttered, scratching my cheek. "I can't help it. Your mum won't laugh, will she?"

"Probably. Hang on, you wait here and I'll go and tell her to behave herself."

I heaved a sigh as Noah disappeared into the house. Great first impression, I thought.

When Noah emerged again, I managed to get my legs to work, and after him assuring me the dog was out the way, I followed him inside. The house was cluttered. Homely. I noticed family photos all along the wall in the hallway, dog toys strewn across the floor, and when I stepped into the lounge, there were bookshelves full of DVDs and display cabinets bursting with knick-knacks. Lime green paint with stencilled yellow flowers decorated the wall. The large sofa, right in the middle of the room in front of the large TV, was brown faux leather. The place smelled like dogs and coffee.

"All right, love?" Noah's mother sat on the sofa, wearing pink pyjamas, her legs stretched across who I presumed to be Chris, Noah's step-dad. She beamed at me.

Chris pulled his gaze away from the TV long enough to say, "Hell, Noah, you work fast, don't you, eh?"

"He's not my boyfriend, all right?" Noah said. Then to me, "Al, this is my mum, Lynsey, and my step-dad, Chris. Mum, Dad, this is Alistair, who I told you about from Whitecott Manor."

"Hi," I said, offering a smile. I felt like a right lemon standing in the middle of their lounge while they sprawled in front of the TV in their jimjams.

"Cor, he's a bit of all right though, isn't he?" Lynsey said, looking me up and down. "If I were ten years younger!"

"Twenty, more like," Chris muttered—to which Lynsey gave him a smack on the arm.

I grinned politely.

"You didn't need to be afraid of the dog, love," Lynsey told me. "Wouldn't hurt a fly, old Herc."

"Mum, it's a phobia," Noah said. "Like you with clowns."

"Oh, don't even say that word, No," Lynsey said, shuddering dramatically. "Bleedin' things."

I scratched the back of my neck and winced. Noah grabbed my arm and led me from the room.

"I think Dan's upstairs," he said. Then at the bottom of the stairs, he bellowed, "*Dani?*" before dragging me up with him.

She appeared from a side room I presumed was her bedroom, pulling headphones off her head. I was surprised to see she was white, and it dawned on me she was his half-sister.

She had short dark hair, and big dark eyes just like Noah, and when she grinned, I could definitely see the family resemblance. "Hiya," she said. "You're Al, from that posh manor."

"I am. I don't *actually* live there though." I wondered what exactly Noah had told his family about me.

"I know," she said. "You're the gardener. Noah says you've got great biceps."

"Dan!" Noah exclaimed.

She winked at her brother and laughed. I just hoped I wasn't blushing, though I couldn't help but laugh as well.

"Is that right?" I asked Noah.

"Maybe," he said, flashing me a smile.

"So, you coming to the show tomorrow, Al?" Dani asked me.

"Yeah," I said. "Looking forward to it. Not sure what to expect, really."

"You'll love it," she said. "I'm just running through my tracks again now." She waved an earplug at me. "Better get back to it. I'll leave you guys to canoodle. Nice meeting you, Al."

"And you," I said. She winked at me and disappeared back into her bedroom. "Canoodle, eh?"

"My family are right wind-up merchants," Noah said. "Can't trust 'em with anyone."

I smiled. Just as I wondered if Noah would show me his room, he grabbed my hand and dragged me back downstairs to his parents.

ON SUNDAY I had my dinner with Dad and spent the rest of the day hauling old Christmas decorations down from the loft. When evening came, I waited nervously for Noah to arrive to drive us to Bristol and his sister's show. I'd never even seen a drag queen act before—though I'd heard Lily Savage had performed in Yeovil years ago—and I had no idea what to expect from a drag *king*. I didn't even know women did that sort of thing.

"Now, now," Emmett said, "Don't be sexist." He sat on my sofa with his legs crossed, his face buried in a newspaper. "If a young lady wants to dress herself up as a man and cavort about on stage looking a pillock, she has every right to do so."

"You're not coming," I told him. "Noah will be here soon. You have to stay here."

Emmett lifted his gaze from his paper. "My dear boy, I'm not a dog."

I pulled back the edge of the curtain and peered out into the street.

"I mean it," I said. "I don't want to look like a lunatic in front of anyone."

Emmett chuckled. I spotted headlights and then Noah's white van and I went to grab my coat from the hall and headed outside to meet him. He pulled up and waited for me as I hurried around the front of his van and got into the passenger side.

"Hiya," he said. "All ready?" He gave me the side-eyes as he shoved the van into gear. "You smell nice."

"Thanks," I said, pleased he'd noticed. I'd worn cologne especially for him. "Yeah, I'm ready. I think."

"It'll be a laugh," Noah said. "Honestly."

I nodded. It took just over an hour to get to Bristol and the club Dani was performing at, but I wanted the journey to last longer. Noah had put the radio on and we belted out the campiest tunes together, laughing and grinning like school boys. He told me Tony was never as much fun and the smugness kept me warm right up until we entered the club.

People bustled about inside the building, laughing and drinking. We squeezed past everyone to get to the bar, which stretched along the back of the room. It was dark in there, lit with pink and blue neon lights and not a lot else. Music pumped into the room from speakers on the walls. The place smelled of sweat, booze, and hairspray.

"What you having?" Noah asked, his voice raised so I could hear him.

"I'll have a beer, thanks," I said. I surveyed the room as Noah got the drinks. The room ended with another door and people seemed to be heading that way once they'd got their alcohol. I presumed the stage was through there.

"Is she first on?" I asked.

"Dunno," Noah said, passing me my glass. "We'll wait and see."

We took our drinks and headed through the door into another larger room. There was no stage, as such, but people had created a space around the red curtains at the back of the room, and large speakers sat at each side, indicating some sort of boundary.

We congregated with everybody else. The energy was buzzing, and I wished I could have a turn on stage. I wondered what I would sing as we sipped our drinks and waited for the first act to come on. Something rock, perhaps. Foo Fighters.

The music quietened. Noah touched the small of my back and turned my attention towards the curtains and I nodded to say I was paying attention. A voice came on over the loud speaker.

"Ladies and gentlemen, welcome to Euphoria! Are you ready to meet the finest, the fittest, the most fabulous kings Bristol has to offer?"

The crowd cheered. By my side, Noah put his fingers to his lips and whistled.

"Then get ready to drop to your knees for Mr Tommy Tank!"

When the music started it took me a moment to realise it was a Billy Idol track—'Rebel Yell.' The curtains parted and a man—no, a drag king—burst out onto the stage. He wore a dirty-white vest top, ripped jeans and a short leather jacket. Noah cheered, and caught up in the moment, I cheered too. As he danced, I clapped along to the drum beats with everybody else in the room. Tommy had Billy Idol's mannerisms down to a T, I noticed, when the vocals kicked in and he mimed along to the track. He grabbed the hands of people who reached for him, and when he came close enough to Noah and me, I admit I wondered where his boobs were—then realised that was probably the first time I'd ever looked for boobs.

He performed to two more tracks, 'Mony Mony' and 'White Wedding,' to rapturous applause from the crowd—a good mix of men and women, who all certainly knew how to enjoy themselves.

The next act was Johnny Hammers, and though I'd forgotten that was the name of Noah's sister's act, I soon remembered when he grabbed my arm and almost jumped up and down in excitement.

"This is it!" he said, grinning. "You ready?"

"Definitely!" I laughed.

The lights dimmed. Vocals kicked in over the speakers, *"It only takes a minute girl,"* before awful 90s-style dance music blared out and Johnny Hammers leapt onto the stage. I stared. Dani wore black trousers with quite a notable bulge and nothing on top. I could see her breasts were taped, but she had an impressive six pack which I gawped at as she danced right in front of us.

It was a 'Take That' track. A few years ago, I'd developed a bit of a crush on Mark Owen and the heat rose to my cheeks as I watched Dani.

"Good, eh?" Noah said, nudging me.

"He... she... he's... *wow*," I said.

"He, and oi! That's my little sister you're drooling over." Noah whooped as Johnny Hammers came closer and sang right at us before spinning away. "Good dancer too, right?"

"Yeah, really good!" I agreed.

After a quick costume change, in which Johnny threw on a leather jacket with long fringes, the track 'Do What You Like' started to play. I recalled the music video well—all very homoerotic, with the lads rolling about together in various food stuffs—and Johnny did not disappoint as he smeared his chest with cake and whipped cream.

Noah must've had enough of me staring at his sister, because I knew he'd not been drinking, and he grabbed hold of me and kissed me hard. Surprised, but not complaining, I returned the kiss.

Chapter Twenty-One

ON MONDAY MORNING I sang as I sat outside the potting shed, wiping down my garden tools with linseed oil to stop them rusting. Ray glared at me once or twice when he passed by, but it didn't damage my good mood, and we managed to ignore each other pretty well. I thought about Noah and the kiss. I replayed the way he'd slipped his arms around my waist, how soft his lips were. It was a cold day and my breath came out in a white mist when I laughed at the memory.

"What are you laughing at?"

I jumped at the voice, dropped my oiled rag, and hurried to my feet, trowel in hand. "Noah!" I said, surprised. "What are you doing here?"

"Came to see you, you doughnut," he replied, grinning. "Got a new client to see in the village—lady with a poodle—so thought I'd pop in here first and say hi. Hi."

"Hello." I pulled him close and planted a kiss on his lips, not caring if Ray was nearby.

Noah pushed me away gently. "Haven't got time for that," he said. "Look, I wanna show you something." He reached into his jacket pocket and took out a piece of paper, which he pressed into my hand.

I downed the trowel so I could unfold the paper and read it. It said: *Found you at last. Call me. Tunde.* And then a mobile phone number.

I looked at Noah. "I don't get it."

"It was shoved under my wipers," Noah said, taking the paper back from me. "Tunde. That's my dad's name. My real dad."

"Oh." I didn't know what to say for a moment. Noah stared at the words. "Are you gonna call him?"

"I dunno. That's why I wanted to see you. What do you think I should do?"

"I...think only you can make that decision," I said carefully. "When was the last time you saw him?"

Noah laughed. "When I was two. And I can't remember that. All I know is what mum's told me about him—his name's Babatunde and he's from Nigeria. That's it. Literally."

"Oh." I scratched my cheek with a dirty fingernail. "Well, he said 'found you at last' so he's been looking for you, right?"

"I guess."

"Maybe you should leave it and let him contact you again?" I suggested.

"But what if he doesn't? What if he thinks I'm not interested because I've not called him?"

I shrugged. "You sound interested, so...call him."

Noah rolled his eyes. "You're rubbish, you are. Don't call him. Call him. Right unhelpful."

"Sorry." I reached out and gave his arm a squeeze. "Maybe speak to your mum about it?"

"I don't want to get her involved." He shoved the paper back in his pocket. "I've gotta go. I'll speak to you later, yeah?" He turned from me and walked away before I had chance to agree or kiss him goodbye.

THAT EVENING I was in the middle of cooking my tea when my phone rang. I thought it was Noah, so snatched my phone up, only to be disappointed to see it was just Dad. I answered the phone anyway, tucking it under my chin as I tossed some vegetables into the hissing wok.

"Hey, Dad."

"All right? Wanted to talk to 'ee about Christmas."

I wondered what was happening with Christmas this year. Last year, Dad and I had had a chicken, rather than a turkey as it was only the two of us, and it'd been just as uncomfortable as our Sunday roasts. The only difference was we had a couple of presents each to unwrap and sat at the table wearing daft paper crowns.

"Uh huh," I said.

"You don't mind if Mrs Dillon comes?"

I grabbed a wooden spoon and pushed my dinner around the wok. "Who?"

"Katie Dillon."

I had no idea who he was talking about. Perhaps my silence gave me away because Dad elaborated, "From the shop."

"Oh!" The Welsh lady. I had no idea she and Dad were so friendly. Wait... "Are you seeing her?"

"I quite often see 'er, ah."

"I mean, are you, like, *together.*"

My dad breathed out hard, as if he didn't want to tell me or wanted me to just be okay with it. "She's...a friend," he said. "I invited her for dinner on Christmas day. We're both alone—"

"You won't be alone. You'll be with me." I frowned as I deposited my slightly overdone stir fry onto a plate.

"And Katie. I've invited her, and that's that."

I wondered what Mum would think. Dad must've thought about Mum; he must've considered her feelings before just inviting another woman over on *Christmas* day. Family day. Mum'd loved Christmas.

"Al?"

"Still here," I said. "I guess if you've already invited her then I can't exactly say no, can I?"

Another hard breath, then, "No."

"Well...good. Thanks for letting me know." I took my plate to the table and sat down before cutting the call and chucking the phone by my side.

"Rude," Emmett commented. He sat opposite me, a steaming plate of stir fry in front of him and knife and fork in hand. "Your poor father deserves some happiness."

I shrugged. I was being childish, I knew that, but... "She hasn't even been dead that long! He should...he should wait at least five years or something! Mum *loved* that man."

"You're being ridiculous," Emmett said. "And selfish."

"I don't give a shit." Annoyed, I pushed my plate away, no longer hungry, and got up abruptly to storm out of the room.

I stomped up to my bedroom and closed the door—not that that would stop Emmett—and flopped down on the bed like a sulky teenager. I wanted to call Noah and whinge but didn't think he'd appreciate it given the current situation with his own father. Briefly, I thought about giving Arthur a ring but quickly shook my head at myself. I'd left my phone downstairs anyway, so I wouldn't be ringing anyone.

IT WASN'T UNTIL I was munching on my breakfast that I picked up my phone and noticed I had a missed call from Noah. He'd rang last night when I left my phone downstairs, and cursing myself for missing him, I called him back.

I listened to the phone ring as I shovelled cornflakes into my mouth, wondering if maybe he'd already headed off to work.

"Hiya."

I smiled when I heard his voice. "Hey. Only just seen you tried to call me last night, sorry."

"Oh right."

He didn't sound as cheerful as usual, but I couldn't work out his mood. "You okay?" I asked.

"S'pose." He sighed. "I spoke to me dad last night. Tunde."

"Yeah?" I sat up straighter, lowering my spoon back into the bowl. "How'd it go?"

"All right, I s'pose. Only, I rang you for advice and you didn't answer so...I called Tony."

My heart did an unpleasant little skip and I frowned. "But you and him—"

"We've split up, yeah, but I needed someone to talk to, and you weren't answering so..."

I could almost hear him shrug. "I'm sorry, I didn't have my phone on me... I wasn't ignoring you. I just didn't know—"

"S'alright. Tony's gonna come with me anyway. When I meet him."

"Oh." I blinked. Tony was going to wheedle his way back into Noah's affections; I knew it! "When are you meeting him? I can go with you, if you like? You can tell Tony he doesn't need to worry."

"Meeting him this afternoon at Costa. Tony's taken time off work and everything. Just...I'll call you later, yeah? Have your phone with you."

I nodded and then realised Noah couldn't see me.

"Yeah," I said faintly. "Good luck."

"Thanks." Noah cut the call, and I was left staring at my soggy cornflakes with my phone still pressed to my ear, convinced I'd messed things up before they'd even begun.

Chapter Twenty-Two

AT WORK I couldn't concentrate. I wanted to be there for Noah. He'd said he was meeting his dad at Costa—that had to be the one in Yeovil. I wondered what time he'd be there and if I could drive over and watch from outside in case he needed me...

"You just want to spy on him and Tony," Emmett said. He stood by my side, watching as I turfed a load of rubbish onto the compost heap.

"That's not true," I replied. "All right, it's kind of true. But I still want to know what's going on, you know?"

"He said he'd ring you and let you know."

"Yeah, but..." I sighed and pushed the wheelbarrow back to the shed. "I could take the afternoon off. It's not like there's loads to do here. Ray can handle it. I could just go and see if he was okay."

Emmett pursed his lips and said nothing. I know he didn't approve, but I'd already made up my mind. It wouldn't be *spying* exactly.

I knew Ray was working on repairing one of the stone walls near the arboretum where a branch had snapped from one of the birches and damaged it, and I headed over there to let him know I was going to head off. As I drew nearer, I could hear him speaking to somebody on the phone so I hung back a little to let him finish his conversation.

He had his back to me, a large pile of stones by his side and very little progress done to the wall. He guffawed loudly.

"...Yeah," he was saying, "nice tight pussy. In her twenties, all legal!"

I frowned and pulled a face, pretty sure I did *not* want to hear that conversation.

"At the manor," he continued. "Owners bugger off and the brother takes over.... No, no! Clean girls. You come along with me next time. Monday—"

I cleared my throat loudly, still scowling to myself. Ray almost dropped his phone and turned quickly to see me.

"Gotta go," he mumbled, before he stashed his phone back into his overalls pocket. "What?"

"I'm off," I said, frowning at him. "Doctor's appointment."

"Aids, is it?"

"Fuck off, Ray."

I turned and stomped away. Stupid bastard. Emmett strode by my side.

"What do you suppose he was talking about?" he asked.

"Don't know and don't care." I marched across the lawn and back to my car, fumbling with my keys when I reached it.

"Calm down. You'll be no help to Noah if you're in a temper."

I shot Emmett a look before getting into the car and pulling on my seatbelt. I sighed as he joined me in the passenger seat. "Sorry. Ray just winds me up."

"My dear, you should rise above it."

We sat in silence then as I drove to Yeovil. I didn't bother going home first to change as I wasn't sure what time Noah would be meeting his dad and I didn't want to miss him. Ray had pissed me off and I tried to think only of Noah and how I wouldn't interfere unless it looked like he needed someone.

"There's something going on," Emmett said eventually. "You need to find out what."

I glanced over at him. "What?"

"At the manor. You've seen it yourself, the suspicious activity. Ray's phone call. You need to find out what's happening."

"Can I just do one thing at a time?" I asked. "Noah first."

"Of course. But on Monday we need to follow Ray."

"I'll probably forget by then," I said. But I was curious despite myself. If Ray was up to something dodgy, I'd love to be the one to rat him out to Zara.

I PARKED AT the multi-storey in Yeovil and walked into town. There weren't too many people around—it was a weekday and the weather was pretty cold—and I felt very obvious as I headed towards the Costa coffee shop. I bought myself a newspaper and sat down on the wall opposite the café, I tried to look as if I wasn't watching the place like some sort of criminal or stalker. As I unfolded the newspaper, I glanced towards the café, noticing a few people inside. My heart skipped when I spotted Noah and Tony and a black man who must've been Noah's father move from the counter and take a window seat.

Don't watch them, I told myself, so I forced my attention back to the paper. I found myself wondering how Noah would've introduced Tony. *This is my ex* or *This is my fiancé*.

Noah's father posed an intimidating figure—well built with a shaved head and, I noticed, as he lifted a cup to his lips, very large hands. I watched them, I couldn't help it. Tony smiled like a greasy salesman and Noah, without his trademark grin, looked nervous. I wish I knew what they were saying and, try as I might, I couldn't lip read.

Fifteen minutes passed before Noah's father got abruptly to his feet, gesticulating wildly with his hands. Noah also stood, an angry look on his face, while Tony sat back and folded his arms across his chest. I sat up straight, newspaper forgotten. Noah's father left the café, his face like thunder, and for the briefest of moments our gazes met before I quickly shoved my nose back in the paper.

Once he passed, I lifted my gaze again to see Noah flap an annoyed hand at Tony. He marched to the door and paused, turning back to shout at Tony, "This is your fault! He didn't need to know!"

As Noah made to leave, Tony hurried from the café too.

"You're making a scene," he called. "Just wait and I'll give you a lift home."

"I don't care, Tony, all right?" Noah said. "Leave me alone."

Tony, perhaps wisely, didn't follow Noah, but I abandoned my paper and jogged after him.

"Noah?"

He spun around, his glare only softening into a look of puzzlement. "What are you doing here?" he asked.

"I uh...came to see you were okay. Are you okay? Need a lift?"

"Were you spying on me?"

"No! I just—"

Noah turned away and carried on walking towards the car park.

"Yeah, I'd like a lift," he said, as I caught up with him. "And no, I'm not okay. My dad's a homophobic bastard. I didn't even want to tell him, I wanted him to get to know me first, but Tony brought it up, and then he kept going on about it like he wanted this to happen."

"I'm sure he didn't." I gave Noah's hand a brief squeeze. "Maybe your dad'll get in touch when he calms down."

"Yeah right. He was dead angry. You should've seen his face!" He stopped walking, not knowing where he was going, and I indicated where I'd parked my car. I drove us back to his house, waiting in the car as he got out.

"Do you want to come in?" he asked.

The thought of the dog struck fear into my guts. Noah's grin returned. "S'alright," he said, "Herc's out with Mum. They'll be out for ages."

I blew a sigh of relief and, smiling, got out of the car.

"All right," I said. "Put the kettle on."

There was nobody home at all. Noah made us both a drink and invited me up to his bedroom.

"Still moving stuff back from Tony's," he explained as I took in the boxes around the room. I was secretly pleased to see them—it meant he and Tony were definitely over. "I'm gonna get my own place soon, I reckon."

"Oh yeah?"

He nodded and sat on the bed, patting the space next to him for me to join him. "Yeah. Thought about going back up to Manchester for a bit, but reckon I'll stay round here."

I sat next to him, my mug gripped between my hands. "I'd miss you if you moved away."

Noah grinned and nudged my arm. "That's dead sweet."

"It's true." I shrugged. "My best mate, Freddie, he moved up to London, and I hardly see him now."

"Well, you'll be seeing lots of me." Noah put his mug on the bedside cabinet and leaned back against the headboard. He smiled at me. "Be nice if we were more than friends though."

I gazed at him. I couldn't think of anything to say that wasn't cheesy, so I leaned over and kissed him instead. He moved his hands to my face—soft hands, not rough like mine—and I belatedly thought about putting my mug down.

Then came noises from downstairs, the door opening, Noah's mum calling, "Coo-ey! Anybody home?"

When the dog barked, I jumped and spilt tea in Noah's lap. He swore, I swore, and I patted ineptly at his wet jeans with my hand. "I'm so sorry!"

Noah pushed me away and jumped to his feet. "You've bloody burnt me!" he exclaimed, dropping his jeans.

"I'm so sorry!" I said again. The top of his left leg was red. His boxers were soaked—they were also, I realised, a grin spreading across my face, bright yellow and adorned with Mr Happy from the Mr Men.

"What?" Noah demanded.

"Mr Happy?" I said.

"Yeah? Well, I'm always happy, aren't I? They were a present, all right?"

I laughed before I could stop myself. Noah looked so funny stood before me in his tea-soaked Mr Happy pants with his jeans around his ankles and an indignant look on his face.

"Fuck off," Noah said, but he was grinning too now. "Look what you've done to my duvet an' all, you clumsy bugger."

There was tea all over his duvet. The mug still dripped in my hand, and I apologised yet again and put it with his.

"How can I make it up to you?" I asked, pulling him close.

"Well," he said, resting his arms on my shoulders. "You can take me out at the weekend. And buy all my drinks."

I laughed. "That's pushing it a bit! But all right."

"Yeah?" Noah grinned and kissed me. "You're dead good." He let me go and put on some fresh trousers, much to my disappointment. "Come on, I better tell Mum to put Herc away so we can get you out of here."

"Yeah, I'll let you get cleaned up," I agreed. "Hey, next time you take off your trousers, I want to see something sexier than Mr Happy, okay?"

Noah laughed. "Sod off," he said. "Like you haven't got any embarrassing underpants."

"I haven't!"

"Yeah, yeah. Wait there. I'll go and hide the dog."

I sat back on the bed and waited, smiling to myself as Noah left the room.

Chapter Twenty-Three

WHEN SUNDAY CAME I called a taxi to take Noah and me to a club in Yeovil so we could both drink and not worry. The driver collected me at my house, and then we drove to Noah's to pick him up. I sat in the back of the cab, my stomach oddly knotted with nerves, while I waited for Noah to join me. He bounded down the pavement like an excited puppy—it was a reasonably warm evening for December, but not warm enough for the T-shirt Noah wore.

"Where's your coat?" I asked as he sat next to me. "You'll freeze."

"Didn't want a coat. I'd only lose it," he said. "Anyway, we only have to go from here to the door, and then we'll be all nice and toasty." He put his arms around me and shivered. "You'll have to warm me up until then."

I smiled and hugged him. "I'm sure I can do that."

We nattered all the way to the club, though luckily for the driver, it was only a five-minute drive from Noah's house, and I was already on a high even before I'd got any alcohol in me. I paid the driver and took Noah's hand as we ran towards the door. Luckily, we'd missed the queue to get in, or Noah probably would've frozen to death. It was much warmer inside with all the people around. I paid to store my coat and then Noah dragged me straight to the bar.

"What you having?" Noah asked.

"I thought I was getting them?"

"You're paying for them, yeah." He grinned at me and beckoned the barman over. "I'll have a WKD please, mate."

"Uh, yeah, the same," I said, hooking my wallet from my jeans pocket. I paid for the drinks and let Noah whisk me away to the dance floor.

We drank and danced together to tracks with no lyrics; we kissed and laughed and drank some more until Noah grabbed my arm and pointed past the throng of people and said, "Look! There's your Arthur."

I followed where he indicated and spotted a familiar blond head. Arthur was snogging the face off some other guy, and I grinned a little.

"He's not my anything," I said. "Let's go and say hi."

I touched the small of Arthur's back and he turned, his face a picture of surprise before he gave me a wide smile. "Al! Good to see you!"

"And you," I said.

Noah flashed him a grin and Arthur laughed and said, "Are you two together?"

I glanced at Noah, but he wasted no time saying, "We are, yeah," and hooking an arm around my waist as if claiming me.

"Well, good for you," Arthur said. He turned to his companion. "This is Luca. Speaks very little English but is an excellent kisser. Luca, be a darling and get us some more drinks, would you?"

Luca gave Noah and me a raised-eyebrow greeting before squeezing off through the crowd to do as Arthur asked.

"He's a bit of all right, him," Noah said. "Where'd you two meet?"

"Oh, we've only just met," Arthur said. "Al will tell you I'm not slow in going after what I want." I hoped I wasn't blushing. I was about to ask Arthur after his health when he said, "Weren't you engaged?"

"Called it off," Noah said. "Too many arguments. Better off like this anyway, I'm far too young to settle down."

"Alistair turned your head," Arthur said, grinning at me inanely. "I can't say I blame you. I do hope he's more focused with you in the bedroom department than he was with me."

I cleared my throat loudly and made my excuses to leave for the toilet before Noah asked any awkward questions. I slipped through the crowd and headed to the loo, hoping Arthur would find something else to talk about other than me hallucinating my dead boss.

The toilets stank and the soles of my shoes stuck to the piss-splashed floor. I relieved myself at the urinals and stared at my reflection in the mirror as I washed my hands. Emmett wouldn't appear if I took Noah to bed, would he? He had to give me *some* privacy.

I headed back out to the dance floor, spotting Arthur and Noah through the crowd. They'd been joined by Luca again, and the three of them laughed together. I smiled, but it dropped when I drew close enough to hear what they were saying.

"...terrible singer," Arthur said.

"He cannot be that bad?" Luca said.

Noah was grinning. "He's not that bad," he said. "But he's not as good as he thinks he is, bless him."

He lifted his gaze and our eyes met. I knew he realised I'd heard because his face fell. I shook my head and turned away, pushing my way out as Noah called after me.

"Al, come on. Wait a minute! Al!"

I stormed outside and the cold air hit me, but it wasn't enough to cool my temper. An empty beer bottle bore the brunt and I booted it across the street. A gaggle of youngsters—too young to be out drinking by the looks of them—looked at me and giggled before passing by. I ignored them. I ignored Noah too when he joined me outside.

"Al, you weren't meant to hear that."

I laughed and shook my head. Did he think that made it better?

"I didn't mean to upset you!" He reached for my hand, but I pulled away.

I paced up and down and dragged a hand through my hair. "You think I can't sing."

"I didn't say that, come on. It's just…"

I glared at him. "I'm not as good as I think I am?"

Noah sighed. He took hold of my hand and then held the other one too so I'd be forced to stop and look at him.

"Does it matter?" he asked. "So you're not going to be the next Katy Perry; you're good at other things!"

"Katy Perry?"

"Well, I don't know. Kylie, then."

"You're so gay," I said, sitting my arse precariously on a bollard. "I love singing."

"You can still sing!"

"Just badly?"

"I never said that." Noah took my hand again. "Forgive me?"

"You were laughing about it with Arthur and his skank. About me." The bollard was really cold. I stood up and rubbed my arse. Noah wrapped his arms around himself, and I noticed how he shivered.

"I'm sorry," he said. "Me and Arthur…we was talking about you because we both think you're so great, okay? We could've been talking about anything else, but we was talking about you."

"About how much I suck."

"Don't sulk." Noah pulled me close and wrapped his arms around me. "You're the best singer I know, all right?"

I wondered how many singers Noah actually knew, but I didn't want to fight any more so I nodded and reluctantly put my arms around him. "We should get you back inside, you're frozen."

"I am freezing my nuts off," he agreed. "But I don't want to go back inside. Take me home. Back to yours."

I collected my coat before I called the cab, and Noah and I sat in the back together with our knees touching. My temper had melted away, and all I could think about was getting Noah home. It was as if my entire focus had narrowed to the point where our legs touched, and I was aware of little else during the trip back. When the car stopped outside my house, I practically leapt out and paid the driver my money as fast as I could. Noah laughed and took my hand to drag me to the door.

"Hurry up, it's bloody freezing!" he said as I fumbled with my keys.

I let us in, stopping to hang up my coat. "Do you want a drink? Coffee or anything?"

"Uh, you're joking, right?" Noah said, shooting me an unimpressed look. "I want to get you upstairs."

I could only grin stupidly before kissing him, taking his cold face between my hands and pressing warmth back into his skin. Again I noted how soft his lips were, how strong his tongue. We both reached for each other's belts at the same time and, laughing, realised we'd be better off closer to the bed. I took Noah's hand and led him up to my bedroom before we were working at each other's clothes again. After I kicked my jeans away and pushed Noah onto the bed, I leaned over him to plant kisses across his chest. He squirmed beneath me, before taking off his own jeans and flinging them to the floor. I could see how hard he was under his boxers.

"No Mr Happy pants today then?" I said.

"Come on, you can see how happy I am without that."

I laughed. "Yeah. Pretty happy myself." We kissed again, grinding against each other. When Noah's hand slipped into my boxers, I groaned. "God, I want you so bad."

"Want you too." Noah removed his hand from my cock and drew me close so he could kiss me again. I pulled away to lean over and grab a condom and lube from my bedside drawer.

"I haven't been with anyone but Tony for a while," Noah said.

That made me pause. "All right. You sure you want to do this?"

He nodded and licked his lips. I noticed the way his gaze flicked to the condom in my hand. "Just...don't laugh if I'm rubbish or anything."

I smiled and quickly bit my lip to stop from laughing. "You won't be rubbish." I planted a kiss on his nose and worked my boxers down my legs. Noah removed his too, and I glanced down at him—seeing for the first time how much bigger than me he was.

"Yeah, Tony gave me that look an' all," he said, grinning.

"Can we not talk about Tony?" I kissed him to stop him from saying anything else, at the same time working on the condom. When I pushed a finger inside him, he gasped and pulled away from me.

"Okay?" I asked.

He nodded. "You always a top?"

"Except with Emmett, yeah."

"Really? I guess it's quite kinky if you're a top. Letting your boss fuck you."

"Can we not have a conversation? I mean, I have got my finger up your arse, I'm a bit...distracted."

Noah wiggled beneath me. "Sorry," he said. "I talk when I'm nervous. You can put another one up there if you want."

I couldn't help, but laugh. "This is so romantic," I told him.

Noah laughed too, and we were soon kissing again. When I finally pushed inside him, it was the sweetest feeling, like I was closer to him than I had been to any other man. He wrapped his legs around my arse, drew me deeper, and I pounded into him, the sound of our mingled breaths and the slapping of our skin loud in my ears.

I didn't think about Arthur. I didn't even think about Emmett until we had both spent and I lay back next to Noah, gazing at the ceiling.

Would Emmett be jealous? If he knew.

Noah shifted closer to me and laid his head on my chest. "That was dead nice, that," he said, and I nodded in agreement.

Chapter Twenty-Four

IN THE MORNING, I woke before Noah and I lay in bed for a moment watching him sleep. I didn't want to go to work, I wanted to stay with him all day—I wanted that moment to last for—

"You can't stay in bed all day. You need to get up, go to work, and keep an eye on Ray." Emmett stood at the foot of my bed, dressed in checked pyjamas with a rolled up newspaper under his arm. "Chop chop."

I groaned. "Ray won't even be there yet," I said. "Don't worry. I hadn't forgotten your little mission."

"I didn't think you had." He waved the newspaper at Noah. "I can see why you're taken with the boy. He is rather beautiful."

"Don't mess things up for me, okay? Please? Just...don't watch us shag or anything. You need to respect my privacy." I got out of bed and grabbed my dressing gown, deciding I'd go and get breakfast ready to surprise Noah.

Emmett followed me from the room. "My dear boy, I want you to be happy."

"Well, Noah makes me happy." I stopped in the kitchen, the tiles cold beneath my feet, and put the kettle on. "Do you think he'd like a fry-up?"

"I'd love one."

I turned quickly when I realised it wasn't Emmett who'd responded to see Noah standing in the kitchen doorway wearing only his boxers. He grinned at me. "Are you talking to yourself?"

"No," I said. "Maybe."

"You're a right weirdo." Noah joined me, wrapping his arms around my waist. "I've noticed you do that before, you know. Talk to yourself."

"Comes from living on my own, I guess." I cleared my throat and turned away to get some bacon and eggs from the fridge. "Toast?"

"Cheers."

Noah went to sit at the table. I tried very hard not to make eye contact with Emmett sitting opposite him.

NOAH TOLD ME he would be working at the manor later in the day and that he didn't have any clients beforehand, so I left him to mooch at my place with the promise I'd come and pick him up at lunchtime. I watched Ray for most of the morning, though he didn't seem to be doing anything particularly incriminating, and then spent a good couple of hours helping Zara put up Christmas lights outside the front of the manor. Well, 'help' was a bit of a stretch. I did all the work and Zara directed me.

"Have you got anything planned for Christmas, Al?" she asked me.

I clambered down the ladder, hoping she wasn't about to change her mind on where to put the illuminated reindeer again. "Not really. I'll be at Dad's. You?"

"Me and David are thinking about going to Barbados. You know, get a bit of sun, have Christmas on the beach."

"All right for some!"

She gave my arm a nudge. "You wanna start playing the lottery, Alistair, you never know what could happen."

I smiled. "I don't think I'm that lucky. Anyway, what'd you do without me here, eh?"

"Cheeky bugger."

"Is that everything with the lights?" I asked. "Only, I said I'd go and collect Noah—"

"Mucky Mutts Noah? My Noah? Are you and he...?" She raised her eyebrows at me and gave a whistle.

"Yeah," I said, unable to stop myself from grinning. "We've only just started dating though so..."

"I thought he was engaged?"

"He was," I said. "Not anymore."

"Well, you kept that quiet. Yeah, you go and get him. I'm going to get all the juicy gossip from him while he's grooming the dogs."

I chuckled. "All right. You might be disappointed though." I collected the tools and ladder and returned them to the shed before heading off to pick up Noah.

When I got home, Noah informed me he'd be able to use Zara's grooming equipment as I briefly worried about having to drive to Yeovil so he could get his van. Then I drove us back to the manor, leaving Noah to it with the warning that Zara knew all about us and would probably spend all afternoon quizzing him.

I got back to work, lingering near Ray again, though once more he wasn't doing anything particularly suspicious.

As I lifted the last of the parsnips in the veggie patch, Emmett joined me. "You'll have to stay behind," he said. "Nothing happens until the Scrantons leave."

I sighed. "Can I not just go home and have a nice tea with Noah? Watch some TV, maybe get laid..."

"Absolutely not. Aren't you the least bit curious?"

I shook dirt off the parsnip and put it in the trug with the others. "Yeah, I am," I admitted. "It's just...what if it's something dodgy? Like human trafficking or something? What am I meant to do?"

"You call the police," Emmett said. "Why don't you ask Noah to stay with you if you're frightened?"

"I'm not frightened." But I would ask Noah, I thought.

When evening came and I saw Zara and David leave, I grabbed Noah's hand and walked with him back towards my car. "We have to pretend we're going home," I told him. "But we'll just circle back."

"This is dead exciting, this," Noah said, grinning at me and glancing back at the manor. "We're like spies or something."

I said nothing. I pulled Noah with me, and we sat beneath the trees lining the lane at the side of the manor. A single light shone through the curtains from the library—a light I knew Zara left on just so it looked like somebody was home.

We huddled together in silence for all of five minutes before Noah whispered, "How long do we have to wait?"

I studied the manor, all still and quiet. No cars turned into the drive. "I don't know," I replied. "Probably nothing'll happen."

"Look!" Noah jabbed me in the ribs, though I'd already spotted what he pointed at. A man wandered around near the front of the building, a torch in his hand.

"It's Ray."

"Do you think he's going to break in?"

"I think he's waiting for someone. Joe maybe."

"Shh!" Noah nudged me again, and we watched as a car came down the driveway, headlights bright.

I knew nobody would see us, huddled as we were in the dark near the lane, but I still held my breath. The car pulled up outside the manor and then Joe Scranton exited the vehicle. He appeared to have a very brief conversation with Ray before they both walked to the door.

"He has a key," I told Noah. "I wouldn't bloody give him one. I wonder if Persephone knows what he's up to?"

"That's his girlfriend, right?"

I nodded. The two men entered the manor and all was still again. One by one, lights came on in the other rooms.

"Maybe they just host a party night or something?" Noah said.

"With Ray?"

"Well, I don't know!"

As time passed, more cars turned into the driveway and pulled up outside the manor. Women, often wearing huge coats but bare legs, paired off with the men as they entered. I glanced at Noah—even in the gloom, I could tell he was rapt, staring at the goings-on. When no more cars turned up, I got to my feet.

"Fancy a closer look?"

"Hell, yeah," Noah said, hurrying to join me. "I could knock on the door, right? Pretend I was a guest."

"No way," I said. "Ray would recognise you."

"Why's Ray invited anyway and you're not?"

"I don't know. I don't think it's a party. And if it is, I don't think Zara did the invites."

We reached the manor and slunk along the outside wall until we reached a window. The curtains were drawn but the lights were on and I could hear laughter inside. It certainly *sounded* like a party. As we carried on round, a man exited from a back door, pulling a young woman with him.

"But it's *freezing!*" she exclaimed.

"So I'll warm you up," he replied, pulling her close briefly to kiss her.

I pressed back against the wall with Noah until they disappeared off towards the arboretum. "Try the door," Noah urged me. "Go on!"

I did. My heart rate increased when I realised it was unlocked. I looked at Noah and he flashed me a triumphant grin before practically pushing me inside. We stood in the small entrance hall together while I tried to get my bearings. The library would be down the corridor and to the left. There was a utility room somewhere around there, as well as the study. Before I could think what to do next, Noah took my hand and led me onwards. Loud laughter behind one of the closed doors made me freeze until Noah turned back to me.

"Let's have a look upstairs," he said.

"We are so going to be caught." I sighed but followed him up the stairs anyway, not knowing whether to be disappointed or pleased that the Scrantons had put blue carpet all over what used to be lovely bare stone.

At the top of the staircase, we stopped again and, eyes wide, Noah looked at me. "Sounds like shagging!" he exclaimed.

Grunts and thumps and heavy breathing radiated out of the nearest room. I screwed up my nose. "Keep going."

We slunk down the corridor, and I was fairly certain I could hear people having sex in other rooms too. A door opened as we approached, and I grabbed Noah and pushed him back against the wall, kissing him.

The person, whoever it was, had stopped. I could feel their eyes boring into me, but I daren't stop kissing Noah.

A man's voice said, "You two fancy some group action?"

I pulled away from Noah. The man was in his fifties maybe—he had white hair and a neat beard—he smiled at me.

"Sod off," Noah said. "This one's not for sharing."

The man shrugged and carried on his way. I laughed in relief. "Bloody hell! We need to get out of here."

"It's like a big orgy party or something," Noah said.

"Do you know what I think?" I said, taking his hand and leading him back to the stairs. "I think Joe's running a brothel."

"No way! Is that illegal?"

"It's very illegal." I glanced back over my shoulder to make sure we were safe and then hurried back outside into the cool night air.

Chapter Twenty-Five

NOAH HAD GONE home as he had a client to get to in Yeovil in the morning, and I lay in bed staring at the ceiling in the half light.

Emmett sat at the end of my bed, dressed in a purple robe. "You absolutely have to involve the police," he said. "I will not stand by and watch Whitecott Manor become a…a cesspit of debauchery and—"

"I don't want to get Zara into trouble," I said. "I'm sure she knows nothing about it."

"She's probably in on it! Why do you think she vacates the premises? So the riff-raff can move in!"

I rubbed my temples. A headache was forming behind my eyes, and I just wanted to sleep. "Maybe I should speak to Persephone."

"I don't want my daughter involved," Emmett said, turning to look at me. "She's pregnant. She needs to avoid stress. I can't believe she got herself mixed up with that…that whoremonger!"

I wondered if I should confront Joe instead. Or Ray—perhaps I could use him somehow, tell him to tell Joe to *stop* or I'd go to the police.

"You need to do something," Emmett said. "Or I will."

I gave a weary laugh. "As much as I would love for you to deal with all this, you can't. You've gone and left me." I rubbed my eyes. When I looked again, Emmett had vanished.

SNOW DRIFTED DOWN from a grey sky, melting as soon as it touched the grass. I sat in the potting shed, hugging a mug of tea and wondering if I should just forget about everything until after Christmas. Ray strolled past the window, whistling, and I scowled at him. No wonder he had a spring in his step.

The fact he was so cheerful stirred me into action, and I put the mug down and hurried out of the shed. "Ray, can I have a word?"

He turned to me. "What?"

"I know what you get up to in the manor. Visiting hookers."

Ray blinked and said nothing. Snowflakes settled on his cap. Eventually he said, "Strange fantasies you queers have."

"I saw you," I said, already annoyed. "I know what goes on in there. It's illegal! The Scrantons could get into all sorts of trouble."

"Only if someone says anything." Ray glanced over his shoulder before approaching me. "And you're not going to say anything, are you? 'Cos nobody likes a grass, boy." He snorted. "Maybe Joe'll set you up with some pussy, eh? Might make you feel better."

I rolled my eyes. "Hardly. Look, I like Zara. If you don't tell Joe to stop using the manor, I'll have to speak to her about it, warn her what's going on behind her back. I'll tell her you're involved and you'll lose your job."

Ray's face turned red. I noticed how he clenched his fists by his side, and I braced myself for a punch, determined not to retaliate.

"Nasty little poofter," he spat. "You'll get what's coming to you."

He must've decided against hitting me, because he turned and stomped off across the lawn like a sulky teenager. I relaxed and turned back into the shed, hoping he'd say something to Joe and Joe would get scared and shut the whole operation down.

I felt a little better and the rest of the afternoon passed without incident. When evening came, I spent most of it on the phone to Noah and his inane chattering cheered me up no end. I found myself thinking about Christmas more and more, and almost invited Noah to Dad's, until I remembered the shop lady would be there.

"Christmas is gonna be weird anyway," Noah said. "Without Tony."

My heart sank. I lay back on my bed with the phone pressed against my ear. "You miss him?"

"He was a big part of my life, you know. We were engaged."

I stayed quiet.

"Don't you go getting jealous," Noah said. "I'm with you now, aren't I?"

"Yeah but...I'm not just a rebound thing, am I?"

Noah laughed. "'Course not, you daft sod! Me and Tony...we're just too different, and I don't wanna be with someone who makes me feel like I can't be me. You're not like that!"

"And you like me, right?"

"I *really* like you."

I could hear the smile in Noah's voice and it made me smile too. "Good," I said. "I'll speak to you tomorrow, yeah? I've gotta go to bed, I need to be up early in the morning to head into town before work."

"All right," Noah said. "What are you buying? Are you getting my Christmas present?"

I laughed. "I'm not buying anything! I have a dentist appointment."

"Oh. Poor you. Hope it goes all right. Speak tomorrow!"

"Yeah," I said. "Good night!" I cut the call and stared up at the ceiling. I vaguely wondered what I could get Noah for Christmas.

MY DENTIST WAS situated in a town called Chard, which was a town about three miles from where I lived and didn't contain very much of interest unless you were really into hairdressers or charity shops. So I was very surprised, having exited the surgery probing at my newly filled molar with my tongue, to spot Noah's dad there.

I stood in the street, staring like an idiot as Tunde crossed the road by the guildhall and disappeared into the bank. I suppose the anaesthetic must've addled my brain because I took it upon myself to find out what he was up to—I think the anaesthetic must've been the reason Emmett rode beside me on a unicycle as I crossed the road, but I didn't think too much on that. I hung around outside the bank until he emerged, and then I practically jumped on the poor bloke.

"Tunde?"

He turned to me with a rather intimidating frown on his face. "Do I know you?" he asked.

"I'm Noah's friend. I was with him in Yeovil when he met you—"

"Tony." Tunde's nose wrinkled in distaste.

"No, my name's Alistair. We didn't meet... I was waiting for Noah outside, I gave him a lift home..."

"What do you want from me?"

"I uh..." I wasn't quite sure, now it came to it. "Well. Just a bit surprised to see you here, I guess. Thought you would've gone back to...Manchester, was it?"

"I took on some work in the area while I was looking for my son," Tunde said. "Not that it is any of your business."

"No." I hurried after Tunde when he turned from me and then struggled to keep pace as he strode down the street. "Noah'd like to see you again," I tried. "He and Tony have split up now, so you wouldn't have to put up with Tony being an arse... Noah's still gay though, so..."

I trailed off. Tunde stopped walking. I winced in anticipation of his reaction.

"He would like to see me?"

"Yeah. He just thinks the two of you got off on the wrong foot." Noah was going to kill me. "He *is* still gay though."

Tunde glowered at me. He took my arm and pulled me out of the way of a little old lady trying to get past with her trolley. "Be quiet. You have a big mouth."

"Sorry. I'm a bit spaced—I've been to the dentist. Filling. Nobody cares, though. That Noah's gay, I mean, not that I had a filling."

"I care." He sighed. "I would like to see him again. Can you pass on a message?"

"Okay."

"I will be in the same coffee shop this Saturday at 2pm. If he is there, we can talk."

"Saturday, 2pm." I nodded. "Got it." I almost threw a salute, but the frown on Tunde's face convinced me that wasn't a good idea. He scowled at me some more and then turned and continued on his way.

I wondered how I was going to break the news to Noah.

"YOU WHAT?"

I sat at the kitchen table on the phone to Noah. My pizza was rapidly going cold in front of me. I winced. "You don't *have* to go. I just thought you might want another chance—"

"Another chance? He's a homophobe, all right? You had no right to arrange that. You can't just meddle in my life!"

"I'm not meddling," I said, affronted. "I thought I was doing something nice."

"Yeah, well you wasn't. You know, Tony used to think he could tell me what to do."

I laughed. "I'm not telling you what to do! You're overreacting." I picked up a slice of pizza and bit into it.

"I don't want to see 'im," Noah said. "Why'd he agree to meet again anyway. I thought he hated me?"

"He doesn't hate you. Obviously he wants to see you." There was silence on the other end of the line. I wiped tomato sauce from my lips. "You don't have to go, but then you'll never know what he has to say for himself. Maybe he's had a change of heart."

"Maybe," Noah said reluctantly.

"If he's still an arse then you've not lost anything by going. I can go with you, if you like?"

"No." Noah answered really quickly and I found myself frowning before he said, "No. Thanks though. I think I'd like to just go on my own, you know? See if we can sort things out properly. And hey, if he is still an arse, I can shout at you some more for arranging the whole thing."

I smiled. "Yeah. Are we good?"

"We're good." Noah changed the conversation then and was soon rabbiting on about something else. I listened and ate my pizza, smiling at how quickly he could get back into a good mood.

Chapter Twenty-Six

I'D MADE SOME blackberry jam back along, and as I had a surplus of it, I grabbed a jar and headed into the village to see old Mrs Harper before Christmas. She ushered me inside, grumbling about letting the cold air into her home, and set off down the corridor using her stick for support.

"All okay, Mrs H?" I asked.

"Hm? Well yes, I suppose so. Apart from the bloody weather. It's not good for my old bones, you know."

I followed her into the lounge, where a fire roared in the hearth, and stopped in the doorway.

"I've got some jam for you. Shall I put it in the kitchen? It's homemade."

"Thank you, yes."

I wandered into the kitchen, put the jam in the cupboard, and made us both a cup of tea before returning to the lounge. I placed old Mrs Harper's cup on the little table by her side where she could reach it.

"You're terribly good, Alistair," she said. "Are you taking over from Arthur?"

"Why, where's Arthur gone?" I asked, frowning that he'd not told me anything.

"Buggered off back to Scotland to spend Christmas with his father," she replied, waving a hand dismissively. "Leaving poor old granny all alone."

"You're not going to be on your own for Christmas, are you?"

"No, no, I'll be seeing Harriet. Which, dire a situation as it may be, is a darn sight preferable to spending the day with the old dears from bridge club."

I chuckled. "Yeah, I don't think that's really your scene." I sipped my tea. "Arthur's coming back, right?"

"I thought you had a new beau?" She gave me a gimlet stare over her glasses. "Though I don't know what on earth was wrong with my Arthur."

"Nothing's wrong with him! And I do, but Arthur's still a mate."

"I approved of you dating my grandson. Lord knows who he'll end up with now. Though it could not be any worse than Persephone's young man."

I grimaced. For a moment I thought about telling her what Joe Scranton got up to at the manor but soon decided better of it.

"He's got her pregnant. Can you believe? Imagine those genes in the Harper line; it doesn't bear thinking about."

"I'm sure there's nothing wrong with his genes," I said.

Old Mrs Harper snorted into her tea cup. "She can do better."

She could do better. God, I hoped Joe hadn't got Persephone mixed up in anything dodgy. We chatted a little more before I made my excuses and headed for home.

Guilt gnawed at me. I felt like I was in on a dirty little secret. My resolve to wait until after Christmas to tell anybody about the manor was failing fast. I had to tell Persephone at least, didn't I? She deserved to know what Joe was doing. But what if Zara and David ended up in prison? What would happen to the manor then? I presumed it'd be repossessed. I could lose my job.

I groaned into my hands. *Wait until after Christmas*, I told myself again. *Things would be clearer then.*

SUNDAY MORNING I spent wrapping Christmas presents. Not that I had many to wrap. I'd bought my dad a bottle of booze, a box of chocolates for the shop lady as I figured I should take her something, an encyclopaedia of dinosaurs for my little cousin, and a bottle of aftershave and some comedy underpants for Noah. I didn't want to buy Noah *too* much in case it made me look clingy, and well, aftershave was pretty expensive.

I'd just finished when there was a knock at the door. I was surprised when I answered it to find Noah on my doorstep. He kissed me and let himself in before I even opened my mouth.

"I thought we weren't meeting until later?" I asked, closing the door and following him through to the lounge.

"Well, I wanted to see you earlier, right?" He pulled me close and kissed me again. "Me and me dad, I think we're all right."

I smiled. "Yeah, you said it went okay yesterday."

"Yeah, but I've been thinking about it. I think we could actually have some sort of relationship, you know? And I've been talking to Mum and Dad—Chris—about it, and they don't mind or anything so... It'll be good, yeah."

"I'm glad." I kissed Noah, and we sat on the sofa together. It wasn't long before we were all over each other, kissing and fondling...there wasn't any time to nip upstairs for the condoms, so we sucked each other off and then lay tangled together half-undressed.

I was comfortable with Noah in my arms, and we were quietly content together until he said, "So have you got my Christmas present or what?"

"I'm not getting you anything." I said it straight-faced to see what his reaction was. He turned and looked at me in horror.

"What, nothing?"

"Nope."

"Well, I've got you something, so that means you have to get me something."

"Does it?"

Noah sat up and his mouth hung open. "Course it does! Do you not know nothing about Christmas? That's the rules."

I laughed. "It's supposed to be more about giving than receiving! And, you know, the whole Jesus thing."

"Shut up. Have you really not got me anything?"

"Course I have. Your face!" I laughed again. "As if I'd not get you anything."

"You're cruel, you are."

"Yeah, evil," I agreed as Noah settled back against me again. We were quiet again for a moment. Then I said, "Come to mine for Christmas dinner."

"I have Christmas with my family," he replied. Then in a softer voice, "And, you know, I kinda wouldn't want Tony to find out; it might upset him."

"Who gives a toss what Tony thinks? Just come in the evening," I tried. "Just for an hour or so. I'd like to see you."

Noah sat up. He swivelled on the sofa to face me, pulling his legs beneath him. "Won't you be with your dad?"

"Please."

“Right, I’ll come, but that means I have to buy your dad a gift so you better give me some ideas.”

“You don’t have to get him anything!”

“Yeah I do.” He leaned back against me again. “Christmas is all about the presents, innit.”

I smiled, pleased he’d agreed so easily. “Yeah,” I said. “All about the presents.”

Chapter Twenty-Seven

CHRISTMAS DAY. WHEN I was little, my mum used to ask me every Christmas morning whether I'd heard the sleigh bells in the night. Of course I hadn't, but she used to tell me she had, and every year I'd try to remember to listen out for them. Thinking of her made my heart ache, so I brushed the memory aside and buried it again.

I'd wished my dad a merry Christmas and we'd eaten breakfast together in silence. Shortly afterwards, Katie Dillon from the shop arrived, and I hung back as my dad greeted her. The warmth on his face when he looked at her made me want to make an effort for him, but at the same time, a little voice inside my head said *you do not get to replace Mum.*

She greeted me with a big smile and a wrapped gift, which was clearly a bottle of alcohol. "Merry Christmas, Al," she said. "Something smells nice!"

"Merry Christmas. Turkey's in the oven," I said. "Can I get you a drink?"

"Ooh, I'll have a white wine if you've got one, please."

I nodded. Exchanged a glance with Dad, catching his *please let everything go okay* look, and disappeared into the kitchen. I put my gift on the table and peered into the oven briefly to make sure nothing was burning or going horribly wrong before fetching the drinks for everybody. Katie's laughter floated through to me from the lounge, and I wondered what Dad had said to her that she could find funny.

As I turned with wine glasses in each hand, Emmett stepped into the kitchen. He wore a Santa suit, complete with red hat and fake beard—which he pulled down, presumably so I'd recognise him.

"Merry Christmas, my dear boy," he said. "Do try to smile. It's the season of merriment and good will and all that."

"I'm just missing Mum, that's all. I'll put on a smile and do all the Christmassy stuff in a minute, don't worry."

I took the drinks through to the lounge and passed them over to Dad and Katie before heading back to pour one for myself. Emmett stood by my side at the work counter, fiddling with the white fluff around his sleeves.

"Damned costume is awfully uncomfortable," he commented.

"Take it off," I suggested.

"Yes, you'd like that, wouldn't you? Not an appropriate time, Alistair!"

I laughed despite myself. I shook my head at Emmett, grabbed my wine and the gift Katie had given me, and returned to the lounge.

"Ready for presents?" I asked, perching myself on the arm of the sofa. "Me and Dad normally do gifts before dinner—if that's okay with you, Katie?"

"Oh! Of course it is, love. When in Rome and all that." She rubbed her hands together gleefully and took the present I offered her. She shook the box theatrically and even said, "I wonder what it could be?" even though it was quite obviously a box of chocolates.

I exchanged a grin with Dad and allowed myself to relax.

As THE HANDS on the clock in the lounge drew nearer to the time Noah said he'd come round, my palms began to sweat. Although I was excited about seeing him, I was also horribly nervous. We'd already experienced some awkward silences during dinner, and while I had to admit Katie was lovely and doing her best to keep conversation flowing, she often had to chatter to herself while Dad and I sat as we usually did, not quite knowing how to interact. I didn't really want Noah to feel any tension.

When the doorbell rang, I jumped to my feet. Dad, who'd been dozing in the armchair while Katie flicked through a book he'd given her, jerked awake and looked at me.

"It'll be Noah," I explained. "I'll let him in."

I rubbed my hands on my jeans as I headed to the door and took a deep breath before opening it. Noah grinned at me.

"Hiya!" he said. He wore a Christmas jumper and carried a bag full of goodies. "You gonna let me in or what?"

I smiled, kissed him, and then let him into the house. "Anything in there for me?" I asked, trying to catch a peek into his bag.

"Might be," he said. "You had a good day?"

I shrugged. "Yeah. You?"

"Yeah, course! It's Christmas. I love it, me." He stuck his head into the lounge and grinned at my dad and Katie. "Merry Christmas!"

"Oh hiya, love, Merry Christmas," Katie replied.

I followed Noah into the room, keeping my hand to the small of his back, wanting to protect him from any weirdness. My dad gave him a nod.

"Had a good day, 'ave 'ee?" Dad asked.

"Yeah, thanks, it's been brilliant. I thought it might be weird, you know, what without my fi—I mean, what without Tony, my ex, but it's been really good. And I couldn't wait to see Al today, so..." He turned and smiled at me, and I smiled back.

"Come and sit down, Jacob," my Dad said.

"Oh, it's not Jacob. It's Noah—"

"It's a term of endearment," I explained quietly, trying not to chuckle even though his sweet naivety made me grin like a loon.

Katie shifted over so we could sit on the sofa together, and Noah clutched his bag in his lap. "Does everybody want presents now, or...?"

"How about I get another round of drinks in?" I suggested. "Then we'll do presents."

I disappeared into the kitchen, trying to be as fast as possible so Noah wouldn't be on his own for too long, but I needn't have worried because when I went back into the lounge, carrying the tray of drinks, Noah and Katie were laughing their heads off at something. Even Dad was grinning from his armchair.

"What's so funny?" I asked, passing the drinks round.

"I was just telling them about last year's Christmas," Noah explained. "Mum spent ages preparing the most amazing turkey, right, and she carved it all up and left it on the table and the dog got to it. Ate the whole damn lot of it. Gave him terrible gas an' all. We had to eat turkey drummers."

I almost said that's why you shouldn't have a dog, but I smiled instead and passed the drinks around before sitting myself next to Noah.

"Come on then, presents," he said, opening his bag. "One for you, Katie, and for you, Mr Ellis, and...here."

I took the gift Noah offered me—it was something soft and flat—most definitely not alcohol or aftershave. "Go on then, open it," he prompted.

Everybody seemed to be waiting for me, so I opened the present. It was a brand new pair of Mr Happy pants. I held them up and laughed. "Mr Happy?"

"You're always singing," Noah said. "And smiling."

I smiled at him. I wanted to tell him it was because of *him* that I was happy, but couldn't bring myself to be such a soppy arse in front of my dad. I checked the label in the pants, impressed he'd guessed my size correctly.

My dad had opened his present by now and made a suitably impressed noise before thanking Noah for his Scotch. Katie opened her gift and seemed quite taken aback. She held her hand in front of her mouth for a moment before saying, "Oh my God, thank you! I lost one of these!"

I peered over at what she was holding—it was a box of small crystal earrings. Noah was clearly better at the whole gift thing than I was; I swear I could see tears in her eyes.

"I noticed a while back when I went in the shop that you had one missing," Noah explained. "Thought you'd lost it and, well, even if you found it again, it's always good to have a spare, right?"

"Thank you so much!" Katie said again, leaning over to hug Noah. "That's so thoughtful."

I beamed at Noah, proud of him. I noticed my dad smiling at him too, clearly impressed.

"Told you I was dead good at presents," Noah said to me. "Can I open mine?"

"Course!"

Noah clutched his presents and then opened them like an eager child. He'd gone for the comedy underpants first and he held them up with a bemused expression on his face. "A potato?"

"It's a hot potato," I clarified.

"Oh right! I don't get it."

I laughed. "I'll explain later. Open the other one."

"Weird that we both got each other undercrackers, though, right?" Noah said, ripping open the other present. "Means we're thinking along the same wavelength or sommat. I can't believe you got me two things though. Well, I can 'cause you think I'm so great but... Oh wow! I bet this was expensive!" He sniffed the aftershave tentatively and then gave an approving nod.

"You like it?"

He leaned over and kissed me. "I love it. Thank you. God, I bet you think I'm a right tight-arse getting you pants."

I held back from making a smutty comment, glanced at my dad, and said instead, "The presents are great, really thoughtful."

"Are you just saying that?"

"No! I love my Mr Happy pants." I gazed at Noah. He was my Mr Happy pants.

LATER IN THE evening, much later, after we'd had a ridiculous and very loud game of Monopoly, Katie made exclamations about the time and left to visit her elderly neighbour as she'd promised the gentleman she would and apparently they had a ritual every year of having a whisky together on Christmas Day. This left Noah and I, and my dad falling asleep in his armchair.

Noah lifted his feet up onto the sofa and rested his head on my shoulder. "This has been dead nice," he said.

"Mm," I agreed, too tired and too lazy to say much more.

"Do you miss your mum?"

My heart did this weird pause thing—it was more than a skipped beat—and when it started again, it was heavy and slow. I frowned, glanced at Dad, and said, "'Course. All the time."

"Must be worse at Christmas though."

I sighed. "Not really. I miss her all the time. It just hurts the most when I think about it."

"Sorry."

I gave Noah's shoulders a squeeze to let him know I didn't mind talking about it. Her. Not really. "If I don't think about it," I said, "I can kinda trick myself into thinking she's still around. After she died, the first few months after, it was still like I was waiting for her to come out of hospital. I felt like I was just waiting for her to come home. There was a weird feeling I'd be seeing her again, like... I knew I'd see her again, but I knew I'd just have to wait for a longer time. And then came the realisation I wouldn't ever see her again, and...and when I think on that..."

Noah pulled back to look at me when I trailed off. From over in his chair, my dad cleared his throat gruffly and said, "Feel like that too, son."

I hadn't realised he'd been listening to me. I wouldn't have spoken if I'd thought he was awake. "I miss her, Dad."

"I know. But she'll be looking down on us, making sure we're all right."

I smiled. "Yeah." Something passed between me and Dad then—an understanding. We'd both experienced my mother dying, but we'd never really shared it until now. We gazed at each other until one of us—I can't remember who—looked away, embarrassed.

Noah folded his arms across his chest. "Bet she was watching you cheat at Monopoly," he said. "Bet she thought you were a right scally an' all!"

I laughed. "I did *not* cheat! You're just a sore loser."

And just like that, any tension disappeared. Dad excused himself and headed off to bed, and Noah and I curled up on the sofa together until we fell asleep.

Chapter Twenty-Eight

I WENT BACK to work in the New Year. I'd had an excellent Christmas, a fun New Year's Eve out on the lash with Noah, and I returned to work with a big smile on my face. I was just checking some frost damage on one of the bay trees by the manor's back door, when David approached me from across the lawn. I stopped what I was doing and gave him a smile, even though he didn't look in the best of tempers.

"Mr Scranton," I greeted him. He didn't like me, so I didn't bother asking if he'd had a good Christmas as I doubt he'd ask in return.

"I want you off my property," he said, his voice low. He didn't give me any eye contact; instead he looked all about as if making sure nobody was seeing us together.

I laughed. "You do know I work here?"

"Not anymore," he said, glaring at me. "You're fired."

"You can't just fire me!"

"I can," David said. "I have. We only need Ray."

I couldn't believe what was happening; it was surely some sort of joke. "I'm a much better gardener than Ray. And I've been here longer."

"Yeah? The Harpers hired you; we didn't. We just got lumbered with you, and Zara was too soft to let you go."

"I want to speak to Zara." I brushed dust from my hands and stepped towards David. "I don't believe this is coming from her."

"She'll say the same as I have. You've got ten minutes to pack your stuff and go, or I'll call the police and have you removed."

I shook my head. "You can't do this. You can't just fire somebody with no warning, I have rights! You... I'll go. But I will speak to Zara." I stomped away before I did or said anything stupid—my hands were shaking by that point and decking David Scranton would've only made the situation much worse.

I snatched up my lunchbox from where I'd left it in the potting shed, looked around for Ray as I was sure he was behind it all somehow, but couldn't find him, so I left as quickly as I could. When I got into my car, Emmett was already there in the passenger seat.

"My dear boy!" he exclaimed. "You can't go down without a fight."

"I'm not going to. I'll speak to Zara. She probably doesn't even know anything about this."

"Are you sure?"

"Yeah." I turned on the engine and pulled out into the lane. There was no way Zara would do that to me, I thought. No way.

I DIDN'T REALLY know what to do with myself at home. I sat at the kitchen table, tapping my phone against my chin. Should I ring Dad? Noah? I almost rang old Mrs Harper but realised there was nothing she could do to help me. Whitecott Manor was no longer under her jurisdiction.

A small voice inside my mind niggled at me, threatening to bring about a panic. *What will you do with no job? You'll lose everything.*

I wouldn't lose my job. He *couldn't* fire me like that. I'd done nothing wrong, and if they were just replacing me with Ray—insane!—then surely they had to let me work my notice. I couldn't be fired.

Eventually I decided to ring Zara's mobile, after first hiding my number so she couldn't tell who was calling. The phone rang for a long time, and I thought she might ignore a withheld number until eventually she picked up.

"Hello?"

The two little dogs barked in the background, making me feel more nervous than I should.

"It's Alistair," I said.

She said nothing for a moment until she shushed the dogs. Then she said, "I don't really want to speak to you, Al."

I rubbed my forehead, not quite understanding what was going on. "David fired me."

"Are you surprised?"

I frowned. "Yes! Am I supposed to have done something?"

"You have been having *sex*," she hissed the word at me, "in *my* house!"

"What the hell?" I stood up and paced the kitchen. "No I haven't. Where did you get that from?"

"Ray said—"

"Ray." I laughed. "He's lying, Zara! Anything that starts with 'Ray said' is bullshit!"

"Don't you swear at me."

"Sorry. But he's *lying*." I sat down again but only for a moment before I began pacing once more. I was too wired. "It's him. Ray. He's the one who's been—"

"He said you'd try to turn it back on him. Who am I meant to believe, Al? Ray, an older gentleman, or you, a young gay—"

"My sexuality has nothing to do with it!" I exclaimed. "And neither does age. He's a dirty old sod. You want to speak to your Joe—he's turned the manor into a brothel!"

Zara fell silent for a moment until she gave a snort of laughter that let me know she didn't believe me.

"Joe entertains business clients occasionally, Alistair. It's a nice setting. I don't appreciate you making up stories like that, okay? I'm sorry it's come to this, but we're done. Don't call me again."

She put the phone down on me before I could even open my mouth to reply. Cursing, I stabbed at my phone until Noah's number came up and I called him.

"Hey," I said when he answered, barely giving him time to say anything else, "I've been fired. I can't believe it! David basically threw me off the property this morning, I've just had an argument with Zara—"

"Wait, babe, slow down. What?"

I went through to the lounge and sat heavily on the sofa. "I've lost my job. I don't know what to do."

"What do you mean you've lost your job? What've you done?"

"I've not done anything! Ray's been lying about me—he told the Scrantons I've been having sex in their house!"

"You haven't, have you?"

"No! He's twisting it because we found out about the brothel."

"Shit. Well, do you want me to talk to Zara? I'll tell her he's a lying bastard."

I leaned back in the sofa and rubbed my forehead. "I don't know what to do. Zara doesn't know about the brothel. She doesn't believe me."

"I'll talk to her. I'll ring her now. Wait there."

He hung up on me. I smiled a little at how sweet he was being fighting my battles, but I felt sick to my stomach. My heart raced and I was full of nervous energy. I stared at the phone waiting for Noah to call back, trying to imagine what he was saying to Zara.

I don't know how long I waited, staring at the screen, but when it flashed up with Noah's name I answered before it even had chance to ring.

"Hello?"

"She's not answering me."

"I bet she thinks I told you to call her. What do I do now?"

"Look, don't panic. I'm due back there to do the dogs in a few days anyway. I'll speak to her then. I'll tell her what we saw; she can't not believe the both of us. I've gotta go, babe, I've got a client in half an hour. Will you be okay?"

I nodded. Then, realising he couldn't see me, said, "Yeah. You go; it's okay."

"All right. Love you."

And he was gone. It took me a moment to realise what he'd said. *Love you*. Had he even realised he'd said it? No, course not. It was just something people said when they ended phone calls, wasn't it? He'd never signed off with that before though.

Love you.

At least I wasn't thinking about my job anymore.

DAYS PASSED. I worked in my own garden and did some odd jobs for my neighbours. I didn't attempt to ring the Scrantons again and I didn't tell my dad what had happened. I just had to keep myself busy and think positive—Zara would see sense and I'd get my job back. And if not... If not then things would be fine. I'd get another job.

Noah came round my house one evening and we curled up on the sofa together in front of the TV.

"Funny thing," he said, as I reached for the remote to change the channel, "Zara never booked an appointment. I was due to see the dogs again, but she never rang."

"So she's sacked you too?"

"She can't sack me. I don't work for her. She's a client." He twisted on the sofa to look at me. "But yeah. Weird, right? She needs her head looking at. We should go to the police, you know, let them deal with it."

"I don't think that's going to get me my job back."

"I'll ring them then," Noah said, sitting up. "I'll do it. Giz your phone."

"No, you can't. We need to get some evidence and show Zara and then she can go to the police herself."

A smile spread across Noah's face. "Yeah?" he said. "Like...what, stake-out or something, you mean? Like cops or spies or sommat."

I chuckled at his enthusiasm. "Yeah, I guess so. Monday evening. You up for it?"

"Course! Sounds dead exciting."

I carried on through the rest of the week with the sole purpose of getting to Monday and vindicating myself and letting Zara know exactly what Ray and her brother-in-law were really like. The fact that Persephone needed to know the true character of the father of her baby also niggled at me, and Emmett told me that several times throughout the week. I told him I couldn't just spring that sort of news on her without evidence—I didn't want her to hate me too—but a part of me was too much of a chicken and was hoping once Zara knew it'd all be out in the open anyway.

On Monday evening, Noah turned up on my doorstep dressed in camo-pants and a black jumper. He wore a black beanie on his head which, he told me, was to help with the concealment. In contrast, I was wearing pale blue jeans and a floral shirt.

"You gotta change for a start," Noah said, squeezing past me into my house. "You can't wear that. You're practically glow in the dark! And have you got some face paints or something? Your skin's whiter than the sun; we need to get you all camo'd up like they do in the army."

I scowled at him.

Noah just rolled his eyes. "Don't look at me like that. Come on." He took my hand and dragged me upstairs. I went without protest, vaguely turned on by him ordering me around.

In my bedroom, I sat on the bed while Noah rummaged in my wardrobe. "Here you are. This'll have to do." He threw a thick brown jumper at me. "And these." A pair of black jeans were deposited in my lap. "Have you got any make-up?"

"Funnily enough, no. My face is fine! We won't be seen."

"Just put those clothes on, will you?"

He stood before me with his hands on his hips, waiting for me to do as he said. I grinned at him. "You are *so* hot."

"Oi, none of that." He moved forwards and put his arms around my neck. "You want to get your job back, don't you?"

"Yeah. Can we not...go in a minute?" I tugged at his waistband to let him know what I wanted, even though I think it was pretty obvious at that stage. "You're being all masterful and sexy."

"Get undressed and put your dark clothes on."

He stepped back and I stood and stripped in front of him.

"Right," he said once I was naked. "Now get your gear on. Come on."

"Noah, come on! There's no rush."

He folded his arms. "Put your clothes on."

I groaned. "This is like horrible, horrible torture. I'm doing what I'm told and I'm getting nothing out of it!"

Noah laughed, and as I turned and bent to get my dark jeans, he slapped my arse. "Just get on with it."

Once I was changed, I headed dejectedly towards the door when Noah said, "Uh, where'd you think you're going?"

"To get my job back."

"Come back here."

I walked back, and as I got near, he drew me in for a kiss. When his hand went to my crotch I moaned into him. It was only a moment before his hand was inside my pants and our breath mingled together as he pulled me quickly to a climax.

I swallowed hard.

"Okay?" he asked, kissing me with his soft lips.

"Uh huh."

Noah grinned. "Good. Can we go now?"

"I've got come in my pants!"

"You're a nightmare, you are." Noah snatched some tissues from the box beside my bed and handed them to me. "Hurry up."

"Mean to me," I grumbled as I cleaned myself up. Noah was already opening the bedroom door.

"Yeah, I'm dead mean," he agreed. "There's no way you would've been able to concentrate with a hard on."

"Yeah, I could. Anyway, you could've fucked me."

"If you stop whingeing, I might do when we get back." He winked at me and disappeared out of the room, calling, "You love it!"

"Tease." He was right, though, I did love it. I dumped the tissues in the bin and followed him out.

THE NIGHT WAS cold, but there was no rain at least. The moon shone silver through a veil of clouds and bats flitted above the trees in the lane as I led Noah from the car. We scurried across the grass together like rats, keeping low and moving quickly. As we drew nearer the manor, I could see no cars in the driveway.

We crouched down behind a box hedge and looked towards the manor. Only one window was on in an upstairs room and the place appeared quiet.

"Maybe we're early?" Noah whispered.

"Maybe."

"Should we get a bit closer?"

Noah made to stand, but a car turned into the driveway, headlights blaring, and I pulled him down quickly.

"That's Joe's car," I said.

We waited, watching, crouched together in the dark. I held my breath as Joe got out of the car and headed towards the manor. He was alone.

"Now what?"

"Wait, I guess," I replied. "When the others arrive, I'll start filming."

Noah nodded. He reached for my hand and gave it a squeeze. "This is dead exciting. I feel like a ninja."

I gave him a quizzical look. "A ninja?"

"Yeah! You know. They're stealthy and that."

I chuckled. "Right. I feel more like a criminal or something, like I'm doing something I shouldn't be."

"Nah, this is good, right? This is what the cops should be doing."

I nodded. Another car drove slowly by, its tyres crunching the gravel driveway. I gripped Noah's hand. After it pulled up and the engine turned off, a man dressed in a dark suit stepped out of the driver's side. He walked around the vehicle and opened the door for a woman—she wore a rather conservative knee-length skirt and flat shoes and didn't look at all how I imagined a prostitute to look. Unless *he* was the prostitute.

"What do male prostitutes look like?" I whispered.

"How am I meant to know that?" Noah nudged my arm. "Get your camera going."

I pulled my phone from my pocket and videoed the couple as they walked to the manor. Joe answered the door after just a brief moment and it was all handshakes and smiles before he invited them in.

"Right, come on." Noah grabbed my hand, pulled me to my feet, and then ran to the manor, keeping low in case anybody was looking out the windows. I hurried after him, though I didn't really know what the plan was.

"The library," I whispered, heading round the side of the building. "We'll have a quick peek in the window."

"And if we can't see anything, we'll have to break in."

I decided talking Noah out of breaking into the manor could wait, and I held up a hand to stop him as I reached the library window. The curtains were open and a light was on. I could vaguely hear muffled voices inside, and I took the chance to sneak a look.

"Well?" Noah prompted.

"They're all in there."

"Are they shagging?"

"No, they're just talking."

"Let me see." He moved past me and peered into the window. "Oh yeah. Wait, the woman's getting up, reckon she's gonna head to the bed—Shit! Run."

"What?"

"Run, they've seen me!" He bolted across the lawn, and I could only curse before racing after him.

Behind me, the window opened and Joe Scranton yelled, "I'm calling the police!"

I caught up with Noah and ran faster. We tumbled out into the lane together, Noah laughing breathlessly, me pretty much shitting myself, though Noah's infectious laughter soon got to me.

"We've got to go," I told him, heading to the car.

"Wait, if he calls the police, then we just tell 'em they're running a brothel."

"There's no proof. They're all just sat there, talking. Fully clothed."

"Oh yeah. Well...now what?"

"We scarper."

I got into the car, waited for Noah to join me, and then drove away.

Chapter Twenty-Nine

THE NEXT DAY, as I was busy painting the door of the village shop as a favour to Katie, a familiar voice behind me said, "Alistair! What *were* you up to last night?"

I turned and smiled at Persephone, hoping I wasn't blushing too much. "Hi. Uh...what do you mean?"

"Joe told me he caught you snooping around at the manor. I hope you weren't going to do something awful."

"Something awful?"

"As revenge for losing your job. Really, Al, if you're going to have sex in your boss's house you can't blame them when they fire you."

"I didn't—" I sighed. Persephone's pregnancy bump was noticeable now and I didn't want to say anything that'd stress her out. "I didn't have sex there, okay? That's just Ray talking nonsense because he doesn't like me."

"Really? What a horrid thing to do. You ought to stand up for yourself."

I bent down to balance the paintbrush on the edge of the tin. "I've tried speaking to Zara; she won't believe me."

Persephone touched my arm and gave me a sympathetic smile. "I'll have a word," she promised. "Don't snoop around the manor again. Joe told me his clients were awfully upset; they thought you were trying to break in."

"Clients?"

"Very important clients," Persephone said. "He just had to have the meeting at the manor. It looks fair more impressive than our little place. Anyway, Al, I have to dash. I have a meeting with the midwife at twelve."

She walked away before I could question her further, so I called 'Good luck!' after her and returned to my painting.

I'd have to be patient if I wanted to catch Joe's brothel at work, I realised. And especially now that he knew I was watching him—he was bound to keep things quiet until he thought I'd given up. I could be patient.

I'D TAKEN ON a small job at old Mrs Harper's. I'd hated having to ask, but when I mentioned I was free to do a bit of work for her, she seemed more than happy to get me out in the garden and clear out her pond.

As I bent to haul pondweed up onto the bank, planning to leave it there for a while for any creepy-crawlies to find their way back into the water, somebody wolf-whistled behind me.

I turned to see Arthur standing in the doorway, and I smiled widely. He looked great. His blond hair was a little longer than I was used to seeing and his skin—still so deathly pale last time I'd seen him—had a healthy pink flush.

"You're back!" I exclaimed.

He laughed. "Absolutely. Did you miss me?"

"Nah." I stood up and brushed my hands together. "I'd give you a hug but...pondweed hands."

"Would you like tea? I'm just making some for Granny."

"Yeah, go on then," I said. I turned back to my work while he disappeared back into the cottage. It was only five minutes before he was back outside with a mug in hand. I looked at it with a frown. "Not one of the finest."

"As if Granny would allow her bone China in the grubby hands of a gardener," Arthur said, passing the mug over. "She'd have my head on a plate."

I shrugged and sipped the tea. "So, how was Scotland?"

"Terribly dull for the most part," Arthur said, folding his arms and leaning against the doorframe. "Apart from New Year's Eve. I went to a party and met a gorgeous Polish chap called Krzysztof. Abs to die for; you should have seen him."

I smiled. "I'm glad you had fun."

"How are things with you and Noah?"

"Okay," I said. We'd had an argument the previous night—Noah had wanted to go out; I'd said I couldn't afford it.

I must've been frowning because Arthur said, "Just okay? Have you had a falling out?"

"Not really." I peered into the mug at the dregs of tea. "I'm just skint at the moment, you know? He wants to go out and I can't take him anywhere."

"Ah." Arthur smiled at me. "You do know you can have perfectly good fun for free, at home in your own bedroom."

I rolled my eyes, though I was smiling. "We have fun. Noah just...he likes to be spoiled sometimes. I like spoiling him. And we really haven't been out for ages anyway."

"Come out this weekend with me," Arthur said. "I promised Harriet I'd take her out on the lash and find her a new man. If there's a little party of us it'll help spread the cost a bit."

"You know what, that's a bloody good idea." I handed him my mug. "Cheers."

Arthur flashed me a smile, took the mug, and went back inside. I turned back to the pond, feeling pleased.

"ARE WE MEETING Arthur inside or what?" Noah asked, tugging his thin jacket tighter around himself as he walked by my side. I grabbed his hand when he almost crossed the road without looking and waited for a car to go by.

"Inside," I said, carrying on across the road towards the club. People mingled outside, laughing and smoking. The music pulsed out into the street.

"What's Harriet like?"

I thought back to the last time I met Harriet when she was drunk and destroying her grandmother's sitting room.

Before I could say anything, Emmett appeared by my side. "Say something nice. Don't go telling Noah she's a drunk."

"I won't." Then, realising I'd said that out loud, to Noah I said, "Uh, I won't know until we see her. She wasn't herself last time we met."

"Who was she then?"

I looked at Noah and he flashed me a grin. Shaking my head, I took his hand and pulled him into the club.

"Keep an eye out for Arthur," I said, raising my voice over the music.

"I'm going to get a drink," Emmett announced, squeezing off through the crowd. I ignored him, not wanting to look a lunatic in front of Noah.

Noah took my hands and pulled me to the dance floor. "Dance with me first!"

We danced close as the music thumped, the deep base line throbbed through my chest, our hips bumped together, and my arms wrapped around his waist. Part of me wanted to sing along to the track, but I couldn't quite bring myself to sing in front of Noah again. We kissed, his lips warm and oh so soft.

"There you are!" Arthur's voice was loud in my ear. I pulled away from Noah to see him and Harriet both smiling at me, drinks in hand.

"Hey!" We hugged, and I introduced Noah to Harriet. She looked more together—her brunette hair was tousled and lovely, and although she wore a low-cut top to show off her ample assets, she still managed to look classy with her slim-fit black trousers and silver heels. Arthur waved his bottle at me. "Your round, I think."

"Sure," I agreed, hoping he'd get the next, and I weaved through the crowd to get to the bar.

I waited. The bar staff were busy, and I didn't want to push in. Emmett joined me, leaning against the bar by my side. "I think it's lovely that your ex-boyfriend and your current boyfriend get on so well."

"Arthur was never really my boyfriend." Still, I turned and glanced back to where I'd left them. They danced together, Harriet and Noah and Arthur. Noah leaned forwards and said something to Arthur and a small twinge of jealously pushed at me.

"I hope they're not talking about your singing again," Emmett said. "You know I think they were terribly unfair. You have a lovely singing voice."

"Thanks," I muttered. I caught the barman's eye and he gave me a nod to go ahead with my order.

I took the bottles and paid, frowning a little at the complete lack of funds in my wallet.

"Spread the cost and slow down," Emmett advised. "You don't need to get hammered to have a good time." He raised his glass and I clinked my bottle against it before making my way back to Noah.

The night continued—we danced and laughed and drank. Everybody paid for a round and then another until it was my turn again.

"I think I'll just have water this time," I said loudly. "And um...would anybody else like juice or something?"

Noah laughed. "No!" he said. "What are you like? Water. I'll have same again, please."

"And same again for me," Harriet said.

I gave Arthur an imploring look. "How about I get this one?" he said.

"It's all right, it's Al's turn," Noah said. "We can keep up, can't we, babe?"

"Well..." I took Noah's arm and pulled him to one side. "I'm skint," I whispered. "I can't afford any more drinks."

"Here." Noah pulled out his own wallet and pushed a note into my hand. "I don't want them two thinking we're paupers. They're dead posh."

"They don't think like that!"

"I know but...just go and get another round, yeah?"

I sighed and made my way to the bar. I didn't know how to get Noah to slow down. When I took the drinks back, Arthur and Harriet peeled off to chat up a couple of guys they'd spotted.

"Can we just slow down on the drinks a bit?" I asked.

"You can, but I want to get drunk!" He grinned at me. I thought he was already drunk.

"You know I haven't got much money."

"So? I've got cash. Stop worrying about it!"

"I don't want you to have to pay for everything."

"Why not? Just don't worry about it and have fun."

"I can't not worry about it," I said. "If you just slow down some, I can still do my bit and get a round in."

Noah rolled his eyes at me. "I don't want to slow down. You know, don't try to tell me what to do, all right? Tony used to do that. If I want to spend my own money and get drunk, I will do. What's the problem?"

"Fine!" I said, throwing my hands in the air. "I'm just going to drink water from now on and only pay for my drinks."

"Why've you got such a cob on?"

"I haven't!"

"You have, you're being a right mardy arse. I said I'd pay."

Noah turned away from me and sought out Arthur and Harriet. I went to sit at a table alone, scowling to myself. I wasn't angry at Noah, not really. I just hated not being able to pay my own way. Emmett came and sat by my side. "My dear boy, you need your job back," he said.

"I know. I'm working on it." I picked up my bottle and gulped back my drink.

Chapter Thirty

NOAH AND I argued. A little at first and then more and more. We argued about money, about going out, about the police and my job, about dogs—I flat out refused to stay the night at Noah's with the dog there. He spent more time with his father, which, while I was pleased for him, started to feel like a bit of an excuse not to see me. Maybe I was reading into it. I saw Emmett more—Noah caught me talking to him and doctors were mentioned. I refused. I didn't sing. I barely worked. Even my dad told me to sort myself out.

I don't know how long we carried on like that. It must've been a couple months. One evening I sat at home on my own watching some crappy show on TV when my doorbell rang. I checked my phone in case I'd had a missed message from Noah, but there was nothing. I got up, and when I answered the door, my mate Freddie grinned at me.

I laughed, and we hugged. "Bloody hell!" I said. "Could've told me you were down this way."

"Wanted to surprise you. You gonna invite me in?"

"Yeah, course!" I beckoned him inside and wandered into the lounge, grabbing the remote to mute the TV. "What are you doing back here?"

"Got some news." Freddie grinned at me. He looked good—smarter than usual, clean shaven and shorter hair than last time I'd seen him. "I'm getting married."

I gawped at him.

"Yeah. Remember the blonde girl from the pub? She's called Teresa. Great girl. Moved her in with me and popped the question a couple of weeks back—was going to do it on New Year's Eve, but I had a bit of a panic about it all."

"Bloody hell. Let me put the kettle on." I wandered out into the kitchen and Freddie followed after me.

"You still single?" he asked.

"No. I'm seeing someone. Noah. He's a dog groomer."

Freddie laughed. He sat himself at the table and grinned at me. "How's that work with your phobia?"

"He doesn't take me to work with him," I said dryly. "He does have a dog though. Bloody big thing. It's practically a horse."

Freddie laughed again and I rolled my eyes. I passed him a mug of tea, and then we went back into the lounge to sit on the sofa. We spoke about Teresa and Noah and silly things like '*Do you remember that time we got so drunk at the King's Arms that you threw up in a bush and then proposed to a lamppost?*'

It was good seeing him again, and just what I needed. I asked about the wedding, and Freddie suddenly remembered he had an invite for me and leaned forward to pull it from his back pocket.

"Bring Noah," he said.

"I will." I smiled at the handmade invite. "If we're still together by then."

"Defeatist attitude, mate," Freddie said. "Sort yourself out. Do you love him?"

I shrugged. Then sighed and nodded.

"Then get over the dog thing, stop moping, and get your act together."

I opened my mouth to protest, but Freddie spoke again. "Look, my missus was scared of spiders, so she went and did this therapy stuff. Over exposure or under exposure or something. Anyway, point is, they made her start slow by looking at pictures of spiders, worked up to videos, and then got her in the same room as one until eventually she could hold one trapped in a glass."

"I'm not scared of pictures of dogs."

"All I'm saying is, you make an effort with Noah and you'll reap the rewards. Try to pat his dog or something, I'm sure he'll hold your hand."

I glowered at Freddie, though it was actually a pretty good idea. I slurped my tea and decided to mention it to Noah the next time we spoke.

WHEN I SAW Noah again, I told him about Freddie and he seemed pleased to be invited to the wedding. I also broached the subject of me perhaps having a very-brief-you'll-have-to-protect-me meeting with his dog, which he was *definitely* happy about considering the sex we had that night.

So when it came down to it, and despite Emmett sitting in my passenger seat telling me that dogs can sense fear, I grit my teeth and told myself to man-up. We'd agreed to meet at the park near Noah's house—Noah said this was because the dog would be more interested in the sights and smells around it than in me, but I suspected it was so I wouldn't feel trapped and could probably make a run for it if I needed.

I wiped my palms in my jeans. I stayed in my car in the car park, though I'd already seen Noah and he'd spotted me, and took a few steadying breaths to calm my nerves. The dog was bloody *massive*, and I wondered if Noah was strong enough to hold it back if it went for me.

I watched as Noah lifted his phone to his ear and wondered who he was calling until my phone buzzed in my pocket. I pulled it out and answered him.

"Are you coming out or what?" he asked. "He won't hurt you, I promise."

"Yeah, I'm just... I uh... Yeah. One second."

Noah put his phone away, flashed me a grin, and beckoned me over. I got out of my car, my fists clenched by my side, my toes curled.

"Should we come to you or—"

"No! I'll come over." I let out a slow breath and approached Noah. The dog turned as soon as I moved and wagged its tail, and I tried my hardest not to make eye contact. My heart thudded.

"Good boy, Herc," Noah said. The dog licked its lips and I froze. "You gonna come over and pat him?"

"I don't think I can get any closer," I replied, staring at the dog. "He's looking at me."

Noah chuckled. "Do you want us to walk past you a couple of times? If we walk past, then you can join us when you feel ready. I'll keep him on the other side of me. Okay?"

I nodded. I stayed glued to the spot as Noah took the dog and walked up and down in front of me. It reminded me of being a kid at school, watching a skipping rope and waiting to jump in at the right moment.

It took Noah five passes before I finally plucked up enough courage to walk by his side. "This is not too bad," I said, though I was all too aware the dog was on the other side of him.

"Baby steps," Noah said. "It'll be nice if you can just come on a walk with us like this. Do you want to take his lead?"

"No! You said baby steps. This is fine. I can handle this."

We walked around the park together, and Noah nattered on about something I couldn't quite pay attention too. Other dogs played off-lead, though luckily none came too close—I wondered if they were as nervous of Hercules as I was—but I did give an approaching owner and his Jack Russell a wide berth as they came towards us.

"You're doing dead good," Noah said. "You haven't run off screaming yet, so…"

I gave him a reluctant smile. "Thanks. I just need to desensitise myself. You wait, I'll be normal in no time."

Noah leaned over and kissed me, and for the first time, I believed I could beat my phobia.

Chapter Thirty-One

I DON'T KNOW why Tony had to come back into our lives, but he did. It started small. Noah told me he'd bumped into Tony one day in Yeovil town centre and they'd had a nice chat. Then I found Noah texting him, a grin on his face. I trusted him, I really did, and I knew I couldn't exactly say anything when I was still friends with Arthur, but god, it made me jealous.

Noah told me Tony was single and not dating anyone, and I nodded and casually remarked, "You told him you're still with me?"

"'Course I did!" Noah replied, and we left it at that because he was scowling and I didn't want an argument.

I trusted Noah. I didn't trust Tony.

One evening, I was just sitting down to eat my tea when Noah called me. Emmett, sitting opposite me with a napkin tucked into his shirt, waved a hand at my phone. "Aren't you going to answer that?"

I picked up my phone and held it to my ear. "Hey."

"Hiya. So, there's this dog show on at the weekend and I'm gonna be there with a little stall doing some grooming and that. You want to come?"

No. "Uh..." I couldn't think of an excuse. Where was an excuse when I needed one?

"Don't worry, you can stay with me in my little area and there won't be any dogs on the loose."

"Cool. Um. I think I'm working, hang on...let me just check my diary." Even though we weren't in the same room, I still made a pretence of getting up and getting my work diary and flicking through it. "What day is it on?"

"Sunday."

"Ah yeah. Working. Sorry."

"Working doing what?"

"I'm putting in some railings for Mrs Mason in the village. She has a bit of a struggle getting down the path without anything to hold on to." I was doing Mrs Mason's railings on the Monday, but Noah wouldn't find out and the best lies were those nearest the truth.

"Oh. All right. Well, maybe I'll see you in the eve, yeah?"

"Yeah, course!" We had a natter then, and Noah seemed happy enough that I was able to push my guilt aside.

ON SUNDAY I had a roast dinner at my dad's house with him and Katie. It was all very pleasant until Dad asked me where Noah was.

"Some dog show...grooming...thing," I said, putting my knife and fork together on the plate and picking up a glass of water.

"Why didn't you go with him?" Katie asked.

"He's scared of dogs," my dad said.

I sighed. "I'm not *scared*; I just don't like them. Anyway, he's fine! He didn't want me there." Both my dad and Katie stared at me from the other side of the table. I rolled my eyes. "I told him I was working."

Katie sucked in a breath through her teeth. "Not good, that is," she said. "Not good at all. You can't go lying to the poor boy." She stood and collected the plates before depositing them over at the sink. Dad pursed his lips at me.

"I didn't want to go, and I didn't want to hurt his feelings," I said. "All right?"

"Well, it's none of my business," Katie said. "Bread and butter pudding?"

"Please."

"But I will say this, once you start lying to someone, you get into the habit. It'll just get worse and worse."

"It's white lie. I'll go with him next time!"

Katie popped a dish into the oven and returned to the table. She shared a look with Dad and then shrugged her shoulders. I forced myself not to sigh again and instead reached for my glass, feeling like a naughty teenager.

After we'd eaten pudding and sat together in the lounge for a while, letting our food go down, my phone rang, and seeing it was Noah, I got up to answer it.

I closed the door softly and answered the call in the hallway. "Hey," I said. "How's the show going?"

"Hello." The voice which replied sounded smug, and my heart dropped to my stomach. "It's going great. Shame you couldn't be here."

"Tony," I said. "What...why have you got Noah's phone? Where is he?"

Tony laughed. "He's just popped off to get us a coffee. Thought I'd give you a little ring to let you know we're having a nice time."

"What are *you* doing there?" I growled.

"Noah invited me."

My heart thumped. I listened hard, aware I couldn't hear any dogs barking—shouldn't there be dogs barking? What if Noah wasn't really at the show? What if he and Tony...?

I stabbed the end call button on the phone, not waiting for Tony to say anything else. Stomping down the hall, I snatched up my coat before stomping back to the kitchen and sticking my head round the door. "Thanks for dinner," I said, "but I've gotta go. I'm sorry. Thanks!"

I left quickly before they could quiz me, and as I closed the front door, I could hear Katie calling my name. Jealousy and rage and—and *fear* all churned with the roast dinner in my stomach as I clutched the steering wheel. I had to get to the show; I had to see what was going on, if they were even there...

I drove as fast as I dared, vaguely hoping a speed camera wouldn't catch me. Emmett sat in the passenger seat, not doing anything to stop me.

"You should forget this and seek out a nice young man instead," he said. "You don't think Tony's stuck his tongue down Noah's throat by now?"

"Noah wouldn't let him."

"Noah invited Tony. I must say, I'm glad we had none of this drama when we were dating."

I gave him a sideways glance. "Dating? All we did was sleep together."

"And how stress-free and wonderful that was! Take it from somebody who was divorced—relationships are nothing but trouble."

The showground was well signposted and I found it with ease. A man in a high-vis jacket directed me into a field where all the vehicles were parked and waved me to a space next to a four-by-four. Heart racing, I turned off the engine and got out of the car. Music played—some live band I didn't recognise, children screamed in play, and a muffled voice announced something over a Tannoy. I was about to march into the adjoining field where the show was taking place when a dog barked and I froze.

"Now what?" Emmett asked.

"Uh..." I turned and scanned the cars, looking for Noah's van. If it wasn't there, then neither was he.

It took a moment before I realised I was just staring blankly, not seeing anything, my own paranoia clouding my vision. I blinked, rubbed my face, and turned to have a walk around the car park to look for the van properly, when somebody tapped me on the shoulder.

"What are you doing here?"

I turned to Noah, and I couldn't speak.

"Thought you was working," he continued. "Well, it's good that you're here now, but...well, Tony's here and I don't want you two to argue or anything like that—"

"Are you having an affair?" I blurted the words out before I could think them through.

"What? With who?"

"You and Tony."

"Don't be daft!"

"Why are you here with him then? And not me, your *boyfriend*."

Noah gaped at me. "Are you having a laugh? You told me you were working!"

"Yeah well... I'm not now. Tony called me, from *your* phone, what was he doing with your phone? And where is he now, eh?"

"He's watching the stall for me," Noah said, waving a hand in a vague direction behind me. "And I don't know what he was doing with my phone. He was probably winding you up; you should've told him to do one."

Emmett moved at the corner of my vision, folding his arms across his chest. "You should just let him know you're not happy with him spending time with Tony."

"I'm not happy with you spending time with Tony," I said, glaring at Noah.

"Sorry, but you don't get to tell me who I can and can't spend time with. He's a friend—you spend time with Arthur and you don't see me getting all jealous."

"Tony was your fiancé!" I cried. "I don't *like* him. I don't *trust* him."

"And what about me, do you trust me?"

"Yes!"

"Then what's the problem?" Noah shook his head and then pushed past me. "I think you'd better go home, Al. There's too many dogs here for you anyway."

I stared after him, fists clenched at my side. "Dogs are stupid!" I yelled.

He didn't turn around or yell back at me, and I was left feeling rather daft. I cursed myself and then made my way back to my car. Emmett walked by my side.

"You have got one hell of an apology to make, my boy."

"I know," I said. "I'm an idiot." I cursed again and slapped the steering wheel. What the hell was wrong with me?

Chapter Thirty-Two

IT WAS A Monday in early May. I'd be planting tomatoes at the manor and clipping the hedges. I hoped Ray was keeping the place tidy. It was unseasonably warm and I had nothing to do but mow my lawn, and once I'd done that, I sat outside for some time, staring into space. Ray would know to keep the fruit trees well-watered, wouldn't he?

I shook my head at myself and tried not to think about the manor. Instead, I pulled my phone from my pocket and text Noah. Again.

I really am sorry. Forgive me, please? xx

He hadn't answered my last three.

"There will be a thunderstorm later, you mark my words."

I looked up to see Emmett standing over me, holding a beige parasol. He swatted at a bee as it buzzed round him.

"Probably," I agreed, not that bothered.

"You should go to the manor this evening," Emmett said. "Try to catch them in the act again."

I suppressed a sigh and shrugged instead.

"Oh, come on. You can't sit around here moping forever! Prove yourself to Zara, get your job back, and take Noah out somewhere nice to apologise."

"Maybe." I inspected my hands, stained green from where I'd picked up the cut grass without gloves. This time I did sigh, and then I stared into space again.

THE FIRST LOW rumble of thunder came in the early evening. I pulled my attention away from the TV and towards the window when lightning flashed. A moment's silence before the thunder came again, louder this time, and I sat up a little straighter. I had a vague feeling dogs didn't like thunderstorms, so—feeling quite pleased with myself—I took out my phone and sent Noah a quick text.

Thunder here. Hope Herc isn't scared xx

I tapped the phone against my chin, and then, deciding I wasn't going to sit round and wait for his reply, I turned the TV off and got up to grab my coat. I'd take Emmett's advice—snoop at the manor and see if I could catch Joe Scranton running his brothel, and if not, then I'd drive to Yeovil and make sure Noah was okay.

I opened the door just as the heavens opened and the rain came down in torrents. Thunder crashed again, followed by lightning.

"It's only a little rain," Emmett said behind me. "Fetch your brolly."

"Only a little rai—" I stopped when a car pulled up outside my house. I recognised the blonde hair of the driver, and as she opened the door, I gaped as a heavily pregnant Persephone swung her legs out into the rain.

"Don't just stand there," Emmett told me, and I snatched up my umbrella and hurried down the drive to greet her.

"What are you doing here?" I cried, raising my voice as the rain hammered down all around me. "Here, let's get you inside." I held the umbrella over her, and keeping our heads down, we rushed back to my house and safety indoors.

As I discarded the brolly and stood dripping in the hallway, I realised Persephone was crying. Her shoulders heaved and she covered her face with her hands. I froze, not entirely sure what to do until Emmett stepped up and said, "Get her a towel, man!"

"Right! Okay, don't go anywhere." I dashed upstairs and grabbed a clean towel from the bathroom, resisting temptation to dry my own face, before going back to Persephone and handing it over to her. "Are you okay?" I asked. "Stupid question."

"It's Joe," she sobbed, clutching the towel and not doing a lot else with it. "I called him and we argued. I...he...I couldn't..."

I took the towel from her and rubbed her shoulders and arms with it, frowning in concern. "Slow down. What happened?"

She sniffed and took the towel from me then to dry her face and hair. "We had a stupid argument and then he left for work. I just couldn't leave things like that, so I rang him, and he told me not to ring and—"

I steered her towards the kitchen where it was warm and dry. "I'll get you a cup of tea, you sit down."

"—and we argued again, so I thought I'd go and see him because I know he's at the manor today and—and there was this *woman*."

I passed her a mug and sat opposite her at the table. "You think he's having an affair?"

"I think she was a hooker." She clutched the mug and stared at the tea. "I turned straight around and came here. I thought about going to Granny's, but I didn't want her to worry, and I didn't know where else to go."

"It's all right." I turned to Emmett, who was hovering behind me looking worried, and gave him a nod to let him know I'd look after her.

A particularly loud crash of thunder made me jump, and Persephone chuckled a little. "You're not frightened, are you?" she asked.

"No."

She nodded. "I'm sorry. I'm afraid I've dripped all over your floor."

"Don't worry about it." She seemed to calm down a little so I got up. "You just drink your tea and warm up a bit. I'll sort myself out and see if I've got anything dry for you to put on, okay?"

"It'd have to be rather large," she said, patting her belly.

I disappeared upstairs and quickly stripped off to change. I put my PJs on and found a clean T-shirt and a pair of jogging bottoms with an elastic waistband I'd bought to exercise in but had never worn and took it back to the kitchen.

"Here," I said, passing them over. "I'll be in the lounge, okay? Come and join me and we'll have a chat. You can stay here tonight if you need to—I can sleep on the sofa."

"Thank you, Al."

I went into the lounge and sat down with a sigh. The light flickered as the storm raged on outside, and I decided against putting the TV on in case it blew up. I looked at my phone instead, smiling at Noah's text.

He's ok. Thanks xxx

He was talking to me now, at least.

Persephone joined me—she'd changed into the clothes I'd given her, but she didn't look particularly comfortable. She rubbed her belly with a wince as she sat by my side.

"Okay?" I asked.

She nodded. "I just keep getting pains. I think I've upset baby with all this stress."

"Do you need an ambulance or anything?"

"I imagine it's Braxton Hicks that's all. I have them on and off. The baby isn't coming yet, Al."

I didn't know who or what Braxton Hicks was, but I didn't like to ask, so I nodded. I fiddled with my phone and tried not to appear so uncomfortable sitting next to my dead lover's pregnant daughter.

"Thank you for this," she said, reaching over to give my hand a squeeze. "My father would be so pleased you're looking after me."

I glanced at Emmett as he hung back by the TV, wringing his hands and watching Persephone, and I smiled a little.

"Yeah," I agreed. "We got on well, me and your dad."

We chatted a bit then, ignoring the storm outside and the light flickering. I was about to get up to make us another drink when Persephone took a sharp breath.

I frowned. "Another Braxton thing?"

"That felt different," she said. She rubbed her stomach, a grimace on her face. "I'm going to try Joe again. Could you fetch my phone for me? I left it in my bag in the kitchen."

"She's in labour," Emmett said, marching beside me down the hall to the kitchen. "You need to call an ambulance."

"She wants Joe," I said, pulling Persephone's bag from under the table and opening it up. "It's probably not labour, right? Isn't there meant to be waters breaking and screaming?" I fished among tissues and lipstick and a pink coin purse and grabbed Persephone's phone.

"Here," I said, passing it over to her when I returned to the lounge. She took it from me and promptly dropped it on the floor as she doubled over, her face twisted in pain.

I grabbed the phone. "You're not okay, are you? I should call the ambulance."

"Call Joe. Please?"

I sighed and scrolled through the numbers in the directory. I pressed call when I reached Joe's and waited. The phone rang.

Persephone paced in front of the sofa, holding her stomach. She gasped again and gripped the arm of the chair, staying like that until I caught her looking at the clock on the wall.

"They're getting closer," she said. "What's happening?"

"He's not picking up."

Emmett stepped in front of me. "Call the bloody ambulance!"

A sudden rumble of thunder seemed to reverberate through the whole house. Then, lightning flashed behind the curtains, and the light bulb in the ceiling light popped.

Persephone screamed as the room plunged into near darkness. My heart rate sped up and I dialled 999 into the phone before holding it to my ear.

"Nothing's happening." I stared at the phone, realising it'd not even called out. The bars at the top of the screen showed no signal—it didn't even display 'emergency calls only.' "No signal, nothing! What do I do?"

"Get her in the car and take her to the bloody hospital," Emmett said. "She can't have the baby in your living room."

Persephone groaned. "I'm in labour," she said. "Contractions are getting stronger. Why didn't Joe pick up? He's too busy with that hooker; I know he is!"

"I'm going to take you to hospital, okay?"

"I don't want to go to the hospital. I want Joe!" She glared at me—even in the gloom, I could see her eyes flash. She groaned again and paced up and down. "I wanted a home birth. My friend Cecily had a home birth. She had a pool and everything. I wanted a pool!"

"Uh...well, maybe at the hospital—"

"I don't want to go to hospital!"

Thunder crashed. I was way in over my head and had no idea what to do with myself, let alone Persephone.

"Candles!" I said. "I'll get some candles. Don't go anywhere."

I hurried out the room and back to the kitchen, fishing around in the drawers until I found a box of candles and some matches.

"She really should go to the hospital," I told Emmett, aware he'd joined me.

"Good luck convincing her," he said. "She's stubborn like her mother."

"She can't have the baby here."

"I know that!" Emmett waved me away, and I returned to Persephone, showing her the candles, though she barely gave them a look. I put some on the windowsill and some on the mantel and lit them with trembling hands. Briefly I thought of the story I'd have to tell Noah.

"Alistair?"

"Yeah?" I blew the last match out and turned to Persephone. In the eerie candlelight, I could see how her hair plastered to her forehead.

"My waters broken."

I cursed. "Towels, we need towels." I dashed from the room again—my carpet, my poor carpet—and jogged up the stairs to snatch up some clean towels form the airing cupboard. Didn't I need hot water too? Towels and hot water. I didn't know why.

"Here," I said, thrusting a towel at Persephone as I joined her again.

"What am I supposed to do with that?"

"I don't know! I really think we should get you to hospital now."

"I am *not* giving birth in your dirty old car." She gripped my hand suddenly and squeezed hard, puffing and blowing. "It's happening quickly," she said. "I don't think this baby wants to hang around."

I groaned and lay some towels on the sofa. "Lie down or sit down, or... I don't know. Get into some sort of position!"

"I'm not doing yoga, Alistair," she hissed at me. She crouched on her knees in front of the sofa and rested her elbows on the cushions as she rocked backwards and forwards. I dithered behind her.

The room lit up as lightning flashed outside and thunder boomed overhead. Persephone cried out. "I want to push!"

"Well...should you be pushing? Don't you usually have to wait until...something?" I snatched up my phone again, desperately hoping for a signal but finding none. Persephone groaned and I did too, wishing I was anywhere else but there.

"I'll get some hot water." I hurried out of the room and back into the kitchen to boil the kettle. I had no idea what the hot water was for—unless it was to clean my lounge after the inevitable blood bath.

"It's probably for Persephone to clean baby and herself," Emmett suggested. "Try not to panic so. And do hurry back to her; she's all alone!"

I poured water into a large bowl I used for baking—on the rare occasions I baked—and took it back into the lounge. I quickly averted my eyes when I realised Persephone had removed her trousers.

"Al?"

"Yeah?"

"Give me your hand."

I put the bowl down and, glad to be at the head end, I took hold of Persephone's hand. She squeezed hard and screamed, and I winced and fought the urge to pull my hand free from her iron grip.

She puffed, shifted about, gripped my hand even harder, and pushed again. My eyes widened. "Is the baby coming?" I asked.

"Soon!"

I cursed. "You're doing good," I said. "You're..." I could smell burning. Then, from the corner of my eye I spotted the curtains were on fire. Cursing again, I pulled my hand free from Persephone's grasp, grabbed the bowl of water, and threw it over the flames. Smoke spiralled into the air, and I coughed and leaned forwards to open the window.

Behind me, Persephone laughed.

"I'm glad one of us thinks this is funny!" I laughed too though, the whole situation too surreal to do anything else, and joined her again.

I don't know how long passed but it felt like no time at all—to me, at least. I'm sure Persephone felt differently! —before Persephone was telling me the baby was coming.

"Al, help guide the baby," she instructed. Then, when I hesitated, she snapped, "Just get down there!"

The sight of blood and mucus and a bulbous head emerging from between her legs made my stomach turn. I swallowed hard and readied myself to take the baby. Persephone yelled again and I laughed a little hysterically when more of the baby appeared.

"It's coming, it's coming!" I cried. "Push!"

I reached for the baby, gently taking its shoulders and helping it along as Persephone screamed herself hoarse. "It's here," I told her, holding the baby in my hands. "It's—*she's*—here!"

Persephone turned so she could see her daughter, and I wrapped the baby in a clean towel. I wasn't sure what to do about the umbilical cord so I left it well alone and passed the baby over.

Persephone, her face flushed red and sweaty, sobbed in delight as she held her baby in her arms. "Oh Alistair, isn't she beautiful?"

"Beautiful," Emmett agreed, and I nodded and turned to give him a smile.

When the baby began to cry, my own eyes welled with tears and I chuckled at myself. "She's amazing," I said. "Congratulations. Am I... I mean, are we supposed to cut the cord or...?"

"Leave it for the moment." Persephone lifted her top and guided the baby to her breast. It was only then that I realised the storm had stopped.

I sat back and allowed myself to relax a little.

"Al?"

"Mm?"

"What was your mother's name?"

"Samantha," I said.

Persephone lifted her gaze from the baby just long enough to smile at me. "Meet little Samantha Harper."

I sobbed before I could stop myself. "Really? I mean...really?"

"Really. I'm so glad your mother wasn't called Tracey."

I smiled and reached out to touch the baby's cheek. "Hello, Samantha," I said. "Pleased to meet you."

Chapter Thirty-Three

AS SOON I was able to use my phone again—well, and after I'd called an ambulance for Persephone—I rang Noah.

We chattered about the storm and Persephone—I told him I'd managed to set the curtains alight—and I welled up again when I revealed the name of the baby.

"It was amazing," I said. "Totally, totally gross—I mean, I have seen far too much lady parts this evening—but it was incredible. I wish you'd been here."

"Wish I'd been there too," Noah said softly.

There was an odd moment of awkward silence before we both spoke together to fill it. I laughed a little and said, "Sorry, you first."

"It's the competition next month. I want you to be there with me."

"With...the dogs?"

"Yes, Al, with the dogs."

He sounded annoyed, though I'm sure he didn't mean to. I didn't want to go to a show full of stinky, hairy, barking dogs. Could I use the working excuse again? I'd probably been silent for too long because Noah spoke again. "I know you're frightened, all right? But it'll be okay, I promise. I won't leave you anywhere on your own, and you can sit back out of the way so no dogs come near you. I'll look after you."

"I...it's just...when I think of all the dogs around me, I can feel my heart racing. You don't need me there freaking out, it'll put you off!"

"No. it won't! You'll be okay. You'll come and spend some more time with Herc, won't you? We'll get you used to a big dog and the others will be like nothing to you!"

I rubbed my forehead. I could see no way out of this, and Noah obviously really wanted me there.

"Okay," I agreed. "Let me spend time with Hercules first and we'll see how it goes."

"Brilliant." I could hear the grin in Noah's voice and it made me smile. "You're dead good, you are. Right, I gotta go—the storm blew the electrics out here and Mum can't work out how to set the clocks again. She's useless. See you soon!"

The call ended before I had a chance to say goodbye. I smiled and put the phone down. I would get used to dogs for Noah, and I would support him at his competition. Everything would be all right.

I REMEMBER WATCHING the long-tailed tits on the feeders in Mr Fletcher's garden. I'd been kneeling at the borders, pulling up weeds, when two of the little birds flew down—not three feet from where I crouched—and landed on the fat balls. Mum had adored long-tailed tits, and whenever I saw them, I always had a feeling that she was nearby. I was engrossed, so much so that when my phone buzzed in my back pocket, I jumped out of my skin.

I pulled it free and looked at the screen. One message from Zara. Frowning, I opened the message up.

Al, I've spoken to Persephone. A lot has happened. Ray is gone. Call me when you can. I'm sorry.

"Huh." I stood up, frightening the little birds away. Ray was gone? I wondered why Zara couldn't call me herself, unless she didn't want to disturb me at work. I almost didn't call her back, out of principle, but I was too curious.

I held the phone to my ear, idly brushing dirt from the front of my T-shirt.

"Al?" She answered straight away. "I am so sorry. Will you forgive me? Look, I've sacked Ray. Things are up in the air here. Joe...Joe's gone. Poor Persephone. David is...well, we're arguing a lot. He swears blind he didn't know what his bleedin' brother was up to in our house, but...I don't know what to think. My head's all over the place. When I think of all those horrible people on my silk sheets!"

"I'm sorry," I said when she paused for breath. "I did try to warn you."

"I know. I want to make it up to you. I want you to come back to work."

I didn't say anything. *Yes,* I thought. Of course I'd go back to the manor, of course! I scratched the back of my head.

"Well, don't decide yet," Zara said. "I know we treated you terrible. I'll make sure you get a pay rise. If things go bad, between David and me...they won't, but...if they do, I'll make sure you're all right. You're the gardener at Whitecott Manor, no matter what happens."

I couldn't help but smile. "I'll send you a text later, okay? I need to think about it."

"Okay. Thanks, Al."

I cut the call and pushed the phone back into my pocket. Already the birds were returning to the feeder. Mum was definitely watching over me.

NOAH CAME ROUND to mine in the evening, and I pulled him close for a kiss as soon as I opened the door. He pulled back from me, grinning from ear to ear. "You're in a good mood," he commented.

"Yep. Guess who got their job back?"

"You did? That's dead good, that. You must be well pleased."

I took hold of his hand and tugged him towards the stairs. "Let's go and celebrate."

"Wait, I've got Herc in the van."

I froze. "What?"

"I thought if I brought him round here, you could meet him on your own turf and you might feel a bit more comfortable."

Already nerves fluttered in my belly. I swallowed and slowly let go of Noah's hand.

"Shall I bring him in?" he asked.

No. No, no, no, no no. No. My mouth ran dry and I couldn't speak. Noah took my silence as a yes, so he smiled at me and turned back to the door to fetch the dog.

I thrust my hands under my armpits and stood in the hallway, staring at the door. *If it comes near me I'm gonna die.*

The door opened and Noah and the *massive* dog—I forgot how big Hercules was every time—stepped into my hallway. Noah had a hold of the collar, and I could see how the dog strained at it. I clenched my jaw and stared at the dog.

"He's not gonna hurt you, promise," Noah said. "Shall I let him go?"

"No!"

Hercules pricked his ears at that and I just wanted him gone. I was trapped in my own home, in my very small hallway, eyeballing a giant dog-monster.

"Noah, take him out, please. Please. I can't..."

"Calm down. It's okay. Come here, Herc." Noah manoeuvred the dog so he looked away from me. He crouched down and held the dog's head, leaving its backside facing me. "We can try again another time."

I never wanted to try that ever again. "Wait," I said. "Just...keep hold of his head, okay? Don't let him go."

"I won't."

I forced myself to relax, unfolded my arms, and let out an unsteady breath. I inched forwards and held out a trembling hand towards the dog's rump. My vision narrowed as adrenaline pulsed through me. Carefully, my breath held, I touched the dog.

Nothing happened. I don't know what I was expecting, but Herc didn't even turn to look at me. Braver, I gave him a quick stroke.

"That's so good. I'm so proud of you," Noah said, beaming at me. "I knew you could do it!"

I let out a small laugh. "Yeah," I agreed. "This is...okay." I straightened up and stood back. "Maybe you could turn him around again?"

Noah turned the dog, and when Hercules met my gaze, he wagged his tail. "I think he likes me!" I said, weirdly surprised and pleased at the same time. "Can I touch him again?"

"If you want to, don't do anything you don't feel comfortable with, all right? I don't wanna push you."

I nodded. Crouching down in front of the dog, I held out my hand for him to sniff. "Good boy," I said. Hercules licked my hand before I could react. I sucked in a breath and pulled my hand back, my whole body tense.

Noah laughed.

"Shit," I breathed. But then I laughed too.

I don't know what happened. I think for that split second we both let our guard down too much—I should've stood up, Noah should've had a better grip on the collar—Hercules came forwards and bowled into me. I fell back, covering my face with my arms, shouting as Hercules pushed his giant head up under my hands, trying to get to my face. It was too much. I managed to scramble back out the way, heart pounding, and Noah pulled Hercules backwards.

"Get him out, get him out!" I cried. My whole body shook.

As Noah disappeared, taking the dog outside, I dissolved into tears. I couldn't help myself, the shock just hit me, and I curled up against the wall, sobbing. The next thing I became aware of was Noah's arm around my shoulders and his voice—though I couldn't hear what he was saying—soft in my ear.

"Go away," I whispered. I didn't want him seeing me like that.

"It's all right," he said. "I'm so sorry, I—"

"Go away!" I screeched it at him like a man possessed. "I don't want you in here, or your stupid dog, just get out. *Get out!*"

Noah stood up and backed off. I could see I'd hurt him, but at that point in time, I didn't care. I wiped my eyes and got to my feet. "Just go," I said. "Please."

He nodded, turned around, and left. It was a few moments before my legs were steady enough to move me into the lounge, and when I got there, I collapsed gratefully onto the sofa.

Chapter Thirty-Four

NOAH TEXTED ME. Several times. I had missed calls. Missed voice messages. I ignored them all. I wasn't angry with him; I just couldn't face him—I didn't want him to think I was a ridiculous coward. I moped in my room, ignoring Emmett, who sat at the end of my bed with a concerned frown on his face, and wondered if I should just end things with Noah completely. At that point, I felt I was *never* going to get over my dog phobia.

"Do you really want to end it all?" Emmett asked.

I shrugged. No. For me, for my own selfish reasons, I wanted Noah to move out of his mother's and never go near another dog ever again. For him...maybe I should end it, because I couldn't ask him to give up his world.

I tapped my phone against my chin, and then with a sigh, I composed a text message.

Can't make it to comp. So sorry. Please don't be mad. x

Then I forced my sorry self out of bed and went downstairs to make myself something to eat. I turned the radio on and tried to forget about everything.

I RETURNED TO work as if nothing had happened and set about changing some things Ray had done back to the way I had them originally. I noticed police cars outside the manor a couple of times, but Zara assured me everything was okay. David ignored me, so it was business as usual.

Noah and I texted one another and made no mention of dogs or competitions whatsoever. We didn't see each other, but I suppose we were both busy. He told me he was off out with Tunde when I asked if he was free one evening, and when he asked what I was doing at the weekend, I told him I was working. It was true. Sort of. I worked

Saturday, but spent a good deal of the time fending off a reporter who thought—as he couldn't get anything out of Zara—he would follow me around the gardens and ask various questions about the brothel. If I knew about it. If I'd used it. That sort of thing. I glared at him at first and said nothing. Eventually I retreated to the potting shed and locked him out. He took the hint after a while.

On Sunday I had nothing planned but dinner with Dad and Katie. In the evening, I went to the pub on my own. I don't know why—I guess I didn't want to be home in case Noah turned up on my doorstep.

"Coward," Emmett told me as I returned to the table with my pint.

The pub was unusually busy with a group of people dining in for a party, and I felt like even more of a loner weirdo huddled in the corner with my beer. I wiped away the condensation on the glass and ignored Emmett.

"You'll have to see him eventually," he said.

"I will. I still feel like a bit of a dick at the minute."

"He's probably wondering what he's done wrong."

I shook my head. "He knows it's my hang-ups. I'll ask him to come over one evening again and cook him a meal or something."

I lifted the glass to my lips and then stopped when I spotted a very familiar backside park itself up at the bar. Arthur! He hadn't seen me—more occupied with trying to catch the barman's eye—and I almost called out to him to get his attention when another man joined him and put his arm around Arthur's waist.

It was Tony. I gawped at them, my feelings torn between jealously and disbelief. How could Arthur be so daft as to get involved with *him*?

"You know Arthur," Emmett said. "Only interested in sex."

"Yeah, but with *him*?"

I put my pint down and wondered if I could make a quick getaway without being seen. Arthur got up suddenly and headed off to the bathroom, and I turned quickly and pretended to be interested in something out the window. He didn't notice me. Tony, however, did.

I groaned when he said my name, but I forced a smile and looked up. He loomed over me, a smug smile on his face, his thumbs tucked into his expensive jeans pockets.

"Well, well," he said. "Alistair."

"Tony."

"You here all on your own?"

I wanted to lie, but knew I'd look stupid when nobody turned up. "Just fancied a quiet pint," I said.

He chuckled. "I hope you and Noah haven't fallen out. He can be quite high maintenance."

"No, we've not fallen out, and he isn't high maintenance."

"Of course." He smirked, glanced towards the direction of the toilet, and then said, "Looks like we've had a partner swap, doesn't it. Though I knew I'd have Arthur the moment I clapped eyes on him."

I gripped my glass tight to stop my hands from shaking. Tony knew how angry he was making me—it was obvious by the look on his face—but I couldn't help it.

"I love that *thing* he does with his tongue," Tony said. "For such a well-bred young man, he's an animal in the bedroom."

I got to my feet and glared daggers at him. "Arthur's better than you. He'll soon get bored and move on to the next guy."

"Just like he did with you? Don't worry, Al, by then you and Noah will be over and I'll have *you* next."

My cheeks burned and my stupid, traitorous dick twitched at the thought of me and Tony even though I *hated* him. I took a step closer, my heart thumping. "Me and Noah will never be over, so back off!"

"Oh yeah? I know he has a big competition coming up. I also know what you're like with dogs—you wouldn't go to his last show; there's no way you'll go to the big one. Guess who'll step up instead? Me. He'll be so grateful, he'll fall right back into my arms—"

"Fuck you." I pushed past him and made my way towards the exit.

Tony called after me. "You wish!"

Chapter Thirty-Five

ONE WEEKEND NOAH and I finally got together again. We spent the day in Bristol, shopping at first and then watching his sister's show in the evening. We drank too much and had to book ourselves into a Travelodge, where we shagged ourselves senseless and fell asleep tangled in one another. We were both quiet on the drive home—I think we were both still hung-over; I know I felt rotten. I drove us back to mine and once inside, made us both a coffee.

"It's the competition next weekend," Noah said.

I sat next to him on the sofa, leaning forwards to put my mug on the coffee table. Why did he have to bring that up for? I didn't know what to say.

"You sure you won't come?" he asked.

I shook my head. "Sorry."

"I'd really like you there."

"I know, I just…"

I sighed and fell silent.

"You don't have to sigh about it," Noah said. He sounded annoyed.

"I just don't want to talk about it, okay? You know I'd come if I could, but I just *can't*. We had a nice weekend, so let's not ruin it now."

"Fine. Sorry for ruining our weekend." He dumped his mug on the coffee table, sloshing his drink everywhere, and got to his feet.

"Where are you going?"

"Home."

I stood too. "Don't be like that."

"Be like what?" He waved his arms at me. I had no idea how to avoid this argument. "I wanted you with me because you're supposed to be my boyfriend. You know what, even Tony would come with me and he hardly ever supported me! I would do it for you, if you had some big gardening event to go to."

"You don't have a garden phobia!"

Noah laughed. "That's not the point. If I did, I'd *still* go with you because I love you."

I stared at him. He reached out and took both my hands in his, calmer now. "I love you. And I want you with me because I love you. I want to be with you as much as possible; I want to share all these things with you. You feel the same, right? You love me too?"

I looked at my hands in his to avoid looking him in the eye. I wouldn't be able to give Noah what he wanted. I'd never be okay with the dogs, I just... I couldn't do that to him. I pulled my hands gently free from his and shook my head.

"I'm sorry. I don't love you."

I still didn't look at him, but he stood for a moment in front of me, silent. Then he brushed past me and was gone, closing the door with a soft click.

I closed my eyes.

"Oh, Alistair," Emmett said, his voice gentle. "What a bloody fool you are."

RAIN LASHED AGAINST the car window so hard and fast that I soon couldn't see out. I'd left work early, rained off, and decided to stop by old Mrs Harper's on the way home. Only now, I didn't want to get out the car.

"I'm sure you can visit another time," Emmett said, appearing beside me wearing the most ridiculous yellow rain hat. "She doesn't even know you're here."

"I haven't seen her for ages," I said. "I want to find out if she knows about Arthur and Tony. Maybe she can talk some sense into him."

"Arthur's love life isn't any of your business. Or mother's."

Talking about somebody else's love life would save me thinking about my own. I pulled my hood over my head, braced myself, and dashed from the car. I arrived on old Mrs Harper's doorstep soaked to the skin and tapped on the door. She opened it almost straight away.

"I thought that was you sitting out there," she said. "Take your shoes off!"

I removed my shoes and my coat and tried not to drip all over the carpet as I followed her into the lounge.

"Absolutely awful weather," she said. "Can't do a damned thing."

I eyed the sofa, unsure whether or not I was allowed to sit, but old Mrs Harper waved a hand at me to take a seat, and so I perched on the edge and wiped my hands on my jeans.

"I'll make you a cup of tea," she said, heading to the door.

"I can do that."

"No, you sit there. I don't want you dripping all over the place."

I sat, my hands pressed between my knees, and looked around the lounge as old Mrs Harper pottered about in the kitchen. I noticed a new photo on the mantelpiece of baby Samantha and it made me smile.

"Here we are then."

Old Mrs Harper wandered into the lounge carrying a tea tray, which I quickly took from her and set on the coffee table. She sat in her armchair and hooked the slippers off her feet. "Make mine; there's a good chap."

I nodded and poured her tea into the china tea cup before I made my own.

"I heard you're back at the manor."

"Yeah. Zara realised she'd made a mistake and asked me to come back."

A frown settled across old Mrs Harper's brow as she leaned forwards to take the tea cup from me. "I hope you gave her a piece of your mind. You've been at Whitecott far longer than they have. You deserve more respect."

"It's all sorted out now." I sipped my tea. "How's the family?"

"Persephone's got herself into a fine mess—she's ruined herself for other men now, though the baby's a dear little thing. Harriet was sober the last time I saw her, which is an improvement. The twins are currently in Rome, and Isabelle is pregnant again. I do hope it's a boy this time."

I nodded and thought better of mentioning Persephone would be an absolute catch for any guy lucky enough to get her attention. "And Arthur?"

"Oh Arthur." She pursed her lips. "He needs to learn that discretion is the better part of valour. I am not so old as to have lost my wits—I know what my grandchildren are up to. I have nothing against promiscuity, but *not* when one lives in such a small village as this."

"You know about him and Tony?"

"Is that what he's called? I don't bother remembering their names. He has a new one every week."

"Tony's my boyfriend's ex."

She raised her eyebrows at that. "And you don't approve? You must tell me, Alistair, if he isn't suitable."

I was a shameless gossip but I didn't care. I put my tea cup back on the tray. "Remember when I broke my leg? That was Tony's fault."

"Really?"

"He's jealous, possessive, bad tempered—"

"I shall tell Arthur he must find a new beau."

I smiled. "Arthur's not stupid. He'll see it for himself. And anyway, like you said, he'll soon move on to the next one."

Old Mrs Harper scowled at me, and so I cleared my throat and reached for my tea cup again. We both sipped at our drinks in silence, until she got to her feet suddenly and wandered over to the writing bureau.

"I have something for you," she said. "Found it the other day. I've had it a little while, but it absolutely slipped my mind; you must forgive me."

"Oh?"

I sat forward and reached for the letter she handed me, though I froze when I recognised Emmett's copperplate handwriting on the envelope and my name: *Alistair Ellis*.

"Take it," she said, waving it at me.

Tentatively, I took the letter. "I'll uh... I'll open it later." I slipped it into my back pocket and swallowed hard.

Chapter Thirty-Six

I WORKED ALL week, keeping my head down, keeping busy. I didn't hear from Noah, but I didn't expect to. I didn't contact him either, much as I wanted to. Emmett pestered me.

"You're making a big mistake," he warned me. "You're throwing away your chance at happiness for a silly reason!"

I told him, again, that I didn't want Noah to give up anything for me and that I was too much of a coward to fit into his lifestyle. He responded by telling me it wasn't my choice to make.

On Friday evening, just as I was relaxing in the bath, Emmett closed the toilet seat and sat down. He said nothing. At first I tried to ignore him and shut my eyes, but I knew he was there, watching me. Judging.

"What do you want?" I asked. "I don't want to think about Noah."

"Won't you open the letter?"

"Why? You know what it says."

"My dear, you are an awful child. Do stop sulking."

I sat up and ran my wet hands through my hair. "I can't read it," I said softly. "Not yet."

Emmett sighed. I stared at the wall, watching condensation run down the tiles. I don't know how long I stayed like that, but eventually I became aware of the cold bath water and my wrinkly fingers. Emmett had gone. I pulled the plug and got out of the bath, shivering as I wrapped a towel around my waist.

I didn't bother changing for bed; I just towelled myself dry and slipped under the duvet cover. For the first time in quite a while, I felt horribly alone.

When morning came, I rolled over and gazed at the light coming through my curtains. A few birds sang the dawn chorus and I listened to them until they fell silent. Then, I got up, washed and dressed, and sat at my kitchen table, letting my cornflakes go soggy. Emmett's letter lay by my right hand.

I expected him to join me, but he didn't. My phone was also silent—no texts or calls from Noah. I wondered if he'd arrived at the competition yet, or whether he was still on his way. Maybe he'd not even left home yet. A tiny voice in my head almost suggested I could text him and tell him to wait for me, that I was coming after all...until I squashed it before it could form properly. I picked up my spoon. Stopped. Then put it down and took the letter instead.

Alistair Ellis.

I wondered what had possessed Emmett to write to me. There was no way he could have known he was going to die. Curiosity got the better of me and I opened the letter.

My Dearest Alistair,

I am a coward. I cannot bear to stick around and watch Whitecott Manor become the home of someone else. So I am leaving—I would have left already by the time you find this letter, I shouldn't wonder, and I suspect you think terribly of me, but I simply cannot bear it. If I am not with my brother in Scotland, I have gone on to sunnier climes.

Please know that I would take you with me—it is my greatest wish that you could be with me—but I can't take you away from your home to please myself. And so I have left without telling you.

Tomorrow, Mr Daniels will be showing the manor to a Mr and Mrs Scranton. I am assured they will buy the place. I plan to stay only long enough to make sure they keep you on and that Mother is settled in to her new home. I will miss you with my whole heart.

All my love,
Emmett x

I stared at the words, heartbroken at first, and then furious. Emmett had been going to up sticks and leave, just like that! And worse, not even tell me to my face! I almost screwed the letter up. Instead, I swiped out at my breakfast bowl, sending mushy cornflakes and milk all over the floor.

"Emmett!" I roared. "Emmett, where are you?"

The bowl hadn't smashed. I kicked it across the floor and it thudded into the fridge. My toe bloody hurt.

"Emmett!"

He appeared before me. "What on earth are you bellowing for?" he asked.

"You were going to leave me." I jabbed a finger at the letter. "You spoke to me since writing that and you didn't let on at all!"

"Didn't have much of a chance before I died."

"You were never going to tell me." I glared at him, my hands shaking now. "You left me a *letter*? I would've gone with you! We could've left together, I—"

"My dear, it was not my wish for you to give up everything for me."

"It wasn't your choice to make! Isn't that what you said to me? We could've *compromised*. I could've visited. We should've spoken about this. I... I was always going to lose you?"

Emmett shrugged. "If I were alive, what would you do now?"

"I'd go and bloody find you and kick your arse," I said.

"I suggest," Emmett said softly, "that you go and find *Noah*. You think that by taking yourself out of his life you're doing the best for him, but don't you see that he needs to make that decision for himself?"

I cursed. "I'm a bloody idiot."

I dashed out of the kitchen, leaving the mess, and Emmett, and grabbed my jacket and shoes. I hoped Noah was still in Yeovil.

I DROVE TO Yeovil as fast as I legally could, and when I reached Noah's house, I got out of the car and ran up the garden path without even closing the car door.

I knocked on the front door, my heart hammering so hard it actually hurt me. The dog barked and I braced myself, balling my hands into fists by my side. Noah's mum yelled, "*Somebody hold Herc!*" before she answered the door.

I offered her a smile, though I was so nervous I think it came across as more of a grimace. "Is Noah in?"

"You're too late." She crossed her arms and leaned against the doorframe, fixing me with a look of disapproval. "He left early this morning. You know, all last night he was checking his phone, waiting for you to call, and I kept telling 'im, he ain't gonna go, No, he's doesn't care about you."

"I do! I do care. I'm here now." I raked a hand through my hair. "Did he go with Tony?"

Lynsey laughed. "Did he 'eck. He was waiting for *you*."

"I'm going to go now," I said. "I've got to be there with him, I get how big this is for him, I—"

"Do you even know where it is?"

"Uh…"

"It's at the exhibition centre, at Leamington Spa. 'Bout a three-hour drive from here, straight up the motorway. You'd better get your finger out."

I grinned. "I'm going. Thank you!"

THE DRIVE TOOK closer to four hours, as I got stuck in traffic, and with way more cursing than was usual for me, I realised I'd left my phone at home so couldn't even contact Noah to tell him I was on my way. I finally found the exhibition centre and was directed into probably the only remaining empty spot in the car park by a grumpy-looking female attendant in a high-vis jacket.

I parked the car and shoved my keys into my pocket as I stood and surveyed the exhibition centre. Dogs sounded alarmingly close and my heart skittered and thumped. I had no idea where or how I was supposed to find Noah—the centre itself looked like a huge warehouse with giant glass doors. I took a calming breath and steeled myself to face the dogs.

As I walked towards the doors, a plump woman approached from the inside—she had two large fluffy white creatures on leads with her—and struggled with the door. I was torn between turning and walking in the opposite direction or helping her. In the end, my better self won and I stepped forwards to grab the door.

She came out, grinning at me in thanks, the two dog-beasts sniffing and waggling round my knees. I mumbled something, I don't remember what, and slipped inside.

The size of the place left me gaping. It, like the Tardis, was somehow bigger on the inside than it looked from outside. Tables and stalls all relating to dogs—dog grooming, dog feeding, dog clothing—were everywhere, as were the dogs themselves of all shapes and sizes and various degrees of hairiness. I looked beyond it all, to a raised area—I guess the 'stage'—at the back of the building, where I could see people standing over their dogs with clippers in hand. I could not see Noah.

I was vaguely aware of a man's voice announcing something incomprehensible—at least to me—over a Tannoy, as I stood like an idiot scratching my head, my eyes glazed.

Find Noah, I reminded myself, though I just didn't know how. With renewed determination, I set off through the building, keeping my eyes on the people not the dogs—ignore the dogs—and scanning the faces hoping to catch a glimpse of my man. There were *too* many people. Thoughts raced through my head: *set off the fire alarm, get everybody outside and then and then... Just yell Noah's name no, no, it might scare the dogs...don't look at the dogs...shit, there's dog everywhere.... Ask somebody if they've seen him, if they know him, could've shown a photo of him if I'd had my phone...could've phoned him if I had my phone!*

I stopped walking. The place was huge and yet I felt surrounded and trapped—somebody walked by with a little dog that decided to sniff my shoes, causing me to freeze and suck in a breath. My head spun, and I was almost overwhelmed by it all until a persistent voice at the back of my head said, "*Try the toilets; he might be in the loo,*" and I set off again. I managed to spot the sign pointing to the toilets and had just changed direction when a dog on a table nearby, a woman groomed it—I hadn't noticed it that close, barked at me—a gruff, angry bark that made me jump out of my skin. I had to stop again; my legs trembled. The woman spoke to me though I couldn't catch what she was saying. My vision blurred and I passed out.

When I woke up, it took me a moment to realise I was in the organisers' office, with two older gentleman and a young woman peering over me. I sat up on the sofa they'd put me on and rubbed my head.

The woman passed me a glass of juice. "Are you all right now? Are you okay?"

I nodded and took the glass, too embarrassed to do anything but sip the juice until I trusted myself to speak. "Thanks," I said. "Sorry."

"You fainted. You're not diabetic or anything? Do you need anything? Are you here with anybody we can contact for you?"

That brought me to my senses and I got to my feet—worrying the woman, who made a grab for my arm. "I'm okay," I told her. "Can I use the Tannoy?"

The two men exchanged a look and one went to the desk. "I'll call them for you. Who shall we ask for?"

"Wait, can I do it? It's my boyfriend. He doesn't know I'm here. I've been an idiot... I couldn't find him, and then all the dogs...so many dogs...."

I trailed off. The woman peered at my head as if looking for a bump, and I offered her a smile. "I'm okay, I promise. Can I just...?" I waved a hand at the desk and the man stepped back with a resigned look on his face.

"Hold this button," he told me, pointing, "and then speak into the microphone."

"Okay." I pressed the button. For a moment, I was only aware of my heart beat until I began talking. "Noah? It's me. It's Al. I'm here. I can't find you, I looked and then... I fainted." I laughed a little. "It's the dogs. There's so many dogs here! And... I'm bloody terrified, to be honest. I need you to hold my hand. I'm sorry I didn't come with you, I should've left with you this morning, but I'm here now, and if you'll forgive me—please forgive me—come and find me. I'm at the organisers' office. Noah..." I gazed at the microphone. At the back of my mind I knew everybody out in the warehouse would be listening, but all I could picture was Noah's face. "I love you."

I released the button. I'd almost forgotten there were others in the room with me when I turned around to see the men and woman smiling at me. My cheeks burned.

"That was so sweet," the woman said. "Go and see if you can see him coming."

"Thanks." I left my glass on the desk and headed to the door. "Thank you, guys!"

I wandered down the corridor and waited, noticing a few smiles from people nearby as they realised I was the idiot from the Tannoy. Butterflies danced in my stomach, though this time it was at the thought of seeing Noah, not the dogs. If he didn't come and find me...

And then I spotted him through the crowd. He wore the white T-shirt with the navy stripes that I loved so much, and, when our gazes met, he smiled.

He stopped just before he reached me, and I gave him an apologetic half-grin. "Did you really faint?" he asked.

"Yeah. Hit my head. Think I have a bump actually."

As I lifted my hand to touch my head, Noah stepped forward and pulled me into a hug. "You doughnut," he said. "I love you too." He grinned at me then and took hold of my hand. "Come on, we've got, like, literally five minutes until I have to start my clip. I'm going Dutch; remember I showed you in the book? I've got my friend's toy poodle—Tina. That's the dog, not the friend. She's ever so sweet; I'll introduce you."

As I listened to Noah rabbit on, I relaxed. Everything I'd been worried about recently just disappeared and my body felt strangely light. I didn't even flinch when I met Tina. I vaguely wondered if I was concussed.

Chapter Thirty-Seven

WE BASKED FOR a few days after the competition, in Noah's success—winner in the 'experienced' group for the toy poodles, and a special award for 'exemplary handling'—and in each other. I sang—a lot—and we laughed and made love and did all the kind of soppy crap that really annoyed me when I saw it in other people. I didn't see Emmett.

One day, as Noah and I lay in bed together, content in our silence, Noah suddenly said, "You haven't done that thing for a while."

I frowned. "What thing? With the toy? I didn't think you liked that."

"No!" Noah laughed. He propped himself up on an elbow to look at me. "Not that. I mean, I haven't seen you talking to yourself lately."

"Oh." I sighed and lay silent for a moment. Eventually, I sat up. "It's Emmett. I speak to Emmett."

"Your old boss?"

"Yeah." I studied my fingernails. "I miss him."

Noah took my hand and gave it a squeeze. "Did you love him?"

"I did. I do." I pulled free from Noah as the tears came, and I held my head in my hands and cried. I don't know where it came from, and I think it was the first time since he'd died that I'd cried for him. I sobbed harder when Noah put his arms around me and I curled into him.

"I miss him," I managed to say a while after the tears had stopped. "I miss him so much. I want to see him."

"Well," Noah said, still with his arms tight around me, "then we'll go and see him, right? Me and you. We'll go and put some flowers on his grave together."

I hadn't visited Emmett's grave since the funeral. I sniffed and wiped my eyes messily with the back of my hand. "I miss him," I said again, but my voice was just a whisper.

I PLUCKED WHITE and red roses from the path flanking the tennis court at Whitecott Manor, and I trimmed the stems and tied them together with green twine. It was lunch time, though I told Zara I was taking a half day, and I walked back towards the manor and on towards my car in the lane. The sun shone and birds skittered in and out of the hedges. I spotted a green woodpecker leave the line of trees along the lane and fly off across the fields, and as I glanced back to the tree it had flown from, I noticed a group of long-tailed tits.

"Hi, Mum," I said softly, smiling a little.

I opened the car door and put the roses carefully on the passenger seat before getting in and driving back to the village. Noah had promised to meet me at St. Mary's, and as I turned into the quiet road leading to the church, I spied his van in the car park. He must've seen me coming, because he got out of the van to wait for me, giving me a wave as I drew near.

"Hiya," he said, after I parked up and joined him. "You okay? These are nice." He indicated the roses.

"From the manor, Zara said I could take some. Emmett loved the roses."

Noah nodded. We kissed and then headed towards the graveyard together—Noah nattered on about something I couldn't pay attention to. The graveyard was devoid of life besides a ginger cat curled in a sun spot on top of one of the tombs, and it seemed too quiet.

I froze, my heart thumping.

"All right?" Noah asked.

I didn't know. Was I all right? I was about to say goodbye to one of my greatest loves, but I had another by my side. I was *lucky*, I knew that, I understood that, but god, it *hurt*. I was bloody angry too! I'd lost my mother and I'd lost my lover and I was too damn young to have to deal with so much grief. No wonder it drove me crazy.

I laughed. "Emmett would tell me off for being maudlin."

Noah grinned at that. "You do have a right face on you," he agreed. "Come on, let's go and put these flowers down and then get something to eat. I could eat a scabby horse."

We became sombre again as we drew closer to Emmett's grave, and I stepped forwards to lay the flowers by the gravestone. As I straightened up, Emmett appeared before me.

"Right then," he said. "I'll be off."

I nodded. "I miss you."

"My darling boy," Emmett said, "I'd be upset if you didn't."

He smiled at me, tucked his hands into the pockets of his ridiculous purple corduroys, and walked away. Eventually, I could no longer see him.

Epilogue

EVERY SPRING THERE was a fete held on the village green with stalls and bunting and a miniature train ride for the kiddies. The air smelled of hot dogs and candy floss. I gripped Herc's lead tightly as Noah nipped off to the loo, willing the dog not to suddenly decide to chase after anything. Herc groaned and laid his head on his paws, and I smiled and crouched down beside him to pat his head. What had I ever been scared of? Okay, he didn't smell great. And the drool...so much drool. But he was the softest thing.

When I straightened up, I spotted old Mrs Harper taking her purse out of her bag over by one of the cake stalls. I was about to head over when somebody else joined her, and I laughed in delight when I realised it was Arthur. He'd cut his hair short and he wore a kilt—he must've sensed somebody looking at him because he turned and our gazes met.

"Well, well, Arthur Harper," I said as he wandered over to join me with a big grin on his face. "Look at you in your kilt!"

"It's been a while, Al." He held out his hand, and I grasped it warmly.

"How's Scotland?"

"Would you believe I'm missing the place? Or rather, I'm missing a certain someone. Luckily I'm only down here for a week."

"Oh yeah? A new man?"

Arthur smiled. "A wonderful new man. I'm really rather smitten." He reached out to give Hercules a stroke when the dog got to his feet. "Is this your beast?"

"Noah's."

"You two are still an item?"

"Of course!" I looked around for Noah, wondering if he'd got lost on his way back from the toilet.

The miniature train passed behind me on its route around the green, and when Herc pulled forwards, I thought for a moment that he'd chase after it. Panic swelled in my chest, but soon disappeared when I spotted what the dog had seen. Noah rounded a group of children and headed towards me, two sticks of candy floss in his hands.

He grinned widely. "Hiya! Bloody hell, look at you in your kilt."

"That's what I said." I swapped the dog's lead for a stick of candy floss and gave Noah a kiss.

Arthur flushed pink. "I hope I don't look ridiculous."

"You look great," I assured him. I hooked an arm around Noah's waist and took a bite of candy floss.

"I should head back to Granny. I'm sure she'll have plenty for me to carry by now. It was good to see you both again."

"We'll have to go out one evening," Noah said. He grinned wickedly. "Karaoke?"

"Hey, I wouldn't want to embarrass you both with my awesome singing," I said. "Perhaps we could go and see Johnny Hammers perform instead. That's Noah's sister."

Arthur raised his eyebrows. "I see!" He smiled. "I'll invite my new beau down, and we'll make a proper evening of it."

"Sounds good." I shook Arthur's hand again before letting him get back to his grandmother.

"He's dead nice, is Arthur," Noah said as we strolled around the fete together again. "I like all the Harpers really."

I nodded. I loved the Harpers like they were a second family, and I was glad Noah was slowly getting to know each one of them better. I vaguely wished he could've met Emmett, but smiled to myself when I realised how complicated that would've been. As the miniature train passed by again, I did a double take at the driver.

Was he wearing corduroys?

I grinned, took Noah's hand, and listened to him natter on as we headed to the next stall together. Life was good.

About the Author

Emma Jane has been writing stories since primary school, some of which still survive in notebooks in her dad's attic, and wanted to be an author as soon as she realised it was a possible career choice and 'Pony' or 'Ninja' weren't viable options.

Her first short story, Club Freak, about an anonymous woman's determination to find her husband's killer, was published by Park Publication's Debut magazine in May 2009. Since then, she has gone on to write many short stories and poems for various small presses and has achieved an Honourable Mention in the 2011 Writers of the Future competition.

Email: em_jane_82@yahoo.co.uk

Twitter: @emizzy

Website: http://ejtett.weebly.com